DISTANT HEART

By Tracey Bateman

DEFIANT HEART
DISTANT HEART

Coming Soon

DANGEROUS HEART

DISTANT HEART

Tracey Bateman

AVON
INSPIRE

An Imprint of HarperCollinsPublishers

Excerpt from *Dangerous Heart* copyright © 2008 by Tracey Bateman

FIRST EDITION

Interior text designed by Elizabeth M. Glover

Library of Congress Cataloging-in-Publication Data

Bateman, Tracey Victoria.
   Distant heart / Tracey Bateman. —1st ed.
   p. cm.—(Westward hearts)
   ISBN 978-0-06-124634-0
1. Ex-prostitutes—Fiction. 2. Wagon trains—Fiction. 3. Forgiveness—Fiction.
I. Title.
   PS3602.A854D57 2008
   813'.6—dc22   2007038315

08 09 10 11 12 OV/RRD 10 9 8 7 6 5 4 3 2 1

To Vivian Bateman, my precious mother-in-law. You were the exception to the in-law rule, and I cherish the time we spent together. While I wrote this book, you battled illness and won heaven. I look forward to the day I see you again, vibrant, strong, and joyful, waiting for the rest of us with those who have gone on before. You are loved.

One

Toni held her breath, biting back the scream that fought to tear itself from her dry, aching throat. Bronze, nearly naked bodies sat regally, cruelly, atop painted ponies, as fearsome as the masters who rode them. Under a flag of truce these warriors had ridden into camp; wanted to make a trade. And, unless Toni missed her guess, she was the one they had come to acquire.

"Don't worry." Standing next to Toni, her friend and traveling companion, Fannie Caldwell, slipped her trembling hand into Toni's damp palm and nearly squeezed the blood from her fingers. She spoke with a confidence Toni was far from feeling. "Sam and Blake will never let them take you. Even if they have to kill every last one of those half-naked savages."

The words brought little comfort, considering the lecherous stare coming from the one who appeared to be the leader. A thick-chested, flat-stomached man with hair as black as pitch and eyes that gleamed with unmistakable intent. Lust looked the same no matter the color of a man's skin. Toni should know. She'd seen it more times than she cared to remember.

"Looks like they're offering three horses for you." Kip Caldwell, Fannie's thirteen-year- old brother spoke up, obviously impressed. "That's a good offer. That chief is serious as all get out to have you, Miss Toni."

Fannie reached out and gave the boy a hard pinch. "Kip, hush your mouth, for mercy's sake!"

"YOW!" His yelp drew attention from the warriors near the end of the line. They stared, scowled, then turned away. Kip remained belligerent. "You know derned well Blake ain't gonna let her go for that."

"Blake isn't going to let her go at all," Fannie hissed. "You either hush or you can just get yourself inside the wagon. And what have I told you about saying 'derned'?"

"Aw, Fannie. What's wrong with it?"

"Never you mind, just do as I say."

Toni barely listened to the whispered argument as she kept her gaze focused on the bargaining going on a few yards away. She could feel the accusing glares of the other pioneers around her. She could guess what they must be thinking. Once again, the no-good fancy woman had brought danger in their midst. Sweat trickled down her spine, and beneath her arms her dress had grown damp.

Dear Lord, is this what I deserve for all the sins I've committed?

The small band of Cheyenne warriors had been following

the wagon train since daybreak. The wagon master, Blake Tanner, had called a halt at noon and ordered the wagons circled just in case the Indians planned to attack. Only now, in the mid-afternoon heat, had the fearsome creatures ridden into camp with trade on their minds. Given the wagon master's obvious disdain for her, Toni couldn't be as certain as his fiancée Fannie seemed to be that he wouldn't take the opportunity to be rid of her once and for all.

With the firm shake of Blake's head, the negotiations appeared to be reaching a frustrating peak for the chief. He tried to force the reins of three horses into Blake's hands, but the wagon master stepped back, shaking his head again and holding up his hands, palms facing outward. Sam, the half-Sioux scout spoke to the warrior, his tone polite and respectful, but leaving no room for doubt as to the refusal of the Indian's offer.

Nearly weak with relief, Toni swallowed hard and tried to control the urge to vomit. As much as she longed to avert her gaze from the fearsome lot of men with oil-slicked, painted torsos, she felt compelled to look on. She'd heard of the mesmerizing effects of terror that compelled a person to look into the face of a storm or stand unmoving before the dripping teeth of a grizzly bear. But only now had she ever experienced it firsthand.

The Indian loped up onto the back of his horse. He whipped his pony around to face Toni. Terror fused her knees straight and she couldn't have run even if she'd had the presence of mind to do so.

"Woman!" The Indian shoved his finger toward her, then turned it back and thumped his chest. "You come with Swooping Eagle?"

Toni shook her head so fast and vehemently the Cheyenne began to spin before her. The warrior's eyes narrowed to black, glittering slits.

He whipped his pony around once more, his broad, brown back glistening in the beating sun. He held up his arm for the twenty other warriors to follow.

One by one the pioneers lifted kerchiefs and aprons to cover their faces as the horses kicked dust into the dry air in the wake of their departure. Silently, they watched until the last Indian crested a hill on the horizon and disappeared down the other side. Then the buzz began, like a hive of angry bees.

Blake raised both arms and called for quiet. "Listen folks. We haven't seen the last of the Cheyenne. They've been stirring up trouble in these parts for the soldiers and wagon trains for months. It's going to be dark in a couple of hours, so we're going to keep the wagons circled and post extra guards. Especially around the women."

Toni's face burned as slowly the attention of the wagon train folks shifted from Blake to her. "I say we let the chief have her," called Mr. Kane. "I ain't riskin' my neck over some whore."

Fannie gasped and shot into the middle of the circle. "How dare you! Toni can't help what she was before. But she isn't that kind of woman now. So don't you even think about turning her over to that savage. You should be ashamed of yourself for even suggesting such a cowardly thing."

Blake strode forward and placed his arm around his fiancée. "It's all right, Fannie. No one's turning Toni over to the Indians." He pierced Mr. Kane with a look that boded no argument, then scanned the circle. "I want the captain of each section to increase the number of guards per section from two to five. We'll leave six campfires burning and move out at daybreak. No children are allowed to walk without an adult. And at the first sign of any trouble, we'll circle the wagons. Kane . . . keep that pup tied up tomorrow. If he gets loose, I'll shoot him."

Mr. Kane gave a jerky nod, turned and glared at Toni, then stalked off toward his wagon. Slowly the rest of the folks returned to their campsites to begin preparations for what was sure to be a restless night.

Toni's legs refused to move. She watched helplessly as Fannie and Blake walked toward her hand in hand. Her friend reached out and squeezed her hand. "Don't listen to Mr. Kane, Toni. He's just an ignorant, bitter fool. Are you all right?"

"I'm sorry to be the cause of such trouble." Toni felt her lips trembling.

Blake cleared his throat. "I'll leave you two to get ready for the night. We'll post two men outside your wagon. You'll be safe."

"Blake!" Fannie whispered. "Don't you want to tell Toni something?"

Toni placed a hand on Fannie's arm. "It's okay."

"No it isn't." She faced off with her future husband, hands pressed to her slender hips, her legs planted as she glared at him. "Tell Toni it's not her fault that savage took a liking to her."

Blake looked down at his fiancée and spoke in tight-lipped stubbornness. "He likes her hair. If Toni truly wants folks to see her as a changed woman, she should put it up like a decent woman instead of down and blowing in the wind like a . . ."

Fannie gasped, but Toni had expected no less. "He's right." She reached up and began to twist her hair until it rested in a knot at the nape of her neck. "May I borrow some pins, Fannie?"

Fannie's eyes narrowed and she yanked at the pins holding her own hair until it hung free in a mass of riotous red curls. "Here take mine. I won't put it back up until he apologizes to you." So saying, she slapped the pins into Toni's outstretched hand and stomped away to the wagon.

Bewilderment washed over Blake's face, then his lips twisted into a crooked grin. "She sure does have some pretty hair, doesn't she?"

"Yes." Toni smiled.

"I suppose I owe you an apology."

It wasn't exactly the heartfelt remorse Fannie had been looking for, but it was more than Toni expected. "I'll be sure to let her know you said so."

As he walked away, Toni had to wonder how on earth she had ever caught the attention of the chief in the first place. She still had three scars along her cheekbone that had failed to heal properly after the beating she'd taken at the hands of the man who had owned the saloon in Hawkins, Kansas. The saloon where she had entertained any man who met George's price. It was the only life she'd known since she was fifteen years old. Until the wagon train had pushed through the tiny, one-horse town of Hawkins, Kansas, two and a half months earlier, and her life had changed forever. Only now, with her beauty marred, she had thought, truly thought, men would leave her alone. But here she was once again, the object of desire and up for sale.

Sam Two Feathers knew one thing for certain. He'd be hanged before he'd let anyone harm one hair on Toni Rodden's beautiful, white-blonde head. The Cheyenne war chief had been forceful and Sam knew they hadn't seen the last of him. The last couple of hours, he had cautiously scouted along the horizon, looking for any sign to indicate an impending attack. But so far, he'd seen nothing. Most likely they were gathering reinforcements before trying to tangle with a wagon train of 250 members. Sam only prayed the wagon train would reach the fort before Swooping Eagle came back with force.

Darkness had settled over the wagon train and all was quiet, but he doubted anyone could rest after what was the first real threat from hostiles in the months they'd been on the trail since departing from Independence, Missouri, in April.

To be sure, there had been the occasional case of thievery from tribes who were out to cause more mischief than harm.

Pawnee warriors had stolen two cows more than a month ago. And before that five Dakota Sioux warriors had wandered in begging for a meal. They'd eaten more than their share of venison stew and biscuits before leaving on good terms with iron pots tied to leather straps and clanging as they left. Those incidents had lulled the travelers into a false sense of security, despite Blake's and Sam's warnings that they were heading into Cheyenne territory and things wouldn't be as calm from the Indians. But no one had listened. Now they knew better. Hopefully they'd be more on their guard.

Provided all went well, the band of weary travelers would arrive at Fort Laramie tomorrow. Blake had sent a scout ahead to warn the Captain that the train was under threat from the Cheyenne and requested an escort. Hopefully, a company of soldiers was on its way even now to provide extra safety from the disgruntled war chief.

But for tonight, Sam had no intention of taking his eyes off Toni's wagon. Though unlikely, if the Cheyenne did try to sneak back into camp and steal her away, they'd have to go through him first.

Behind him a twig cracked, but he knew it was Blake so there was no cause for action. Blake had been watching the same wagon since the ladies had turned in. "Think we're in for trouble tomorrow?" Sam asked without taking his gaze from the canvas-covered wagon.

"Could be." Blake yanked a twig from his mouth and tossed it to the ground. "I should have known better than to let that woman join this train. This is what I get for going soft."

Sam tried not to let his defenses rise, but Blake could be

coldhearted at times. Although he was getting better since he'd made a decision to follow Christ, and had fallen in love with Fannie, he still had a tendency to be set in his own way of thinking. "The only thing Toni can be accused of is having a beautiful head of blonde hair."

More correctly, hair that flowed like a white waterfall down her back, inviting a man's fingers to swim in the thick currents. He couldn't really blame the Cheyenne warrior. He himself was mesmerized each time the beautiful tendrils floated across her face and even more so, when she unconsciously pulled strands across the scars.

He could feel Blake's questioning gaze on his face and knew his friend had picked up on the direction of his thoughts. He turned and faced the wagon master. "Don't read more into this than it is."

"You care for her."

"I do."

"Then you're a better man than I am."

"All have sinned, Blake. Even you."

Blake gave a short laugh. "She sold herself to men. Nothing I've ever done even compares to that kind of thing."

"Maybe in man's eyes. But sin is sin in God's eyes. Besides, my friend, Fannie, too, was forced to make difficult decisions, was she not?"

Anger flashed in Blake's eyes. "Don't even compare the two. Fannie had no choice. Toni did. She chose to sell her body."

"Perhaps," Sam gave a long exhale, "Toni also felt she had no choice."

"Are we going to let a fancy woman come between us?"

Sam's lips tightened into a grim line. "Only if you insist upon calling Toni words that no longer suit her. God has forgiven her, Blake. What right have you to refuse her a second chance?"

Blake stuck his thumb through his belt loop. "Mark my words, Two-Feathers. That woman will be back in business at the first opportunity that comes her way. And if you lose your heart to her, you're the worst kind of fool."

Sam held his tongue. He didn't need Blake Tanner telling him what kind of fool he was. Sam had lost his heart months ago, the moment he'd laid eyes on Toni. And no matter what anyone thought, he'd play the fool even though he knew she would never be his.

Blake expelled a loud breath. "Everyone turned in?"

Relieved to change the subject, Sam gave a nod. "I think so."

"The Kanes' pup tied up?"

Sam gave a solemn nod. "Yeah, but he's not happy about it. Neither is Zach. And Mrs. Kane's worried the dog's going to hang himself pulling against his rope so bad."

"Too bad. That animal's a menace. It would be a mercy if the ignorant beast did hang himself. We should have left the ornery cuss where we found him."

Sam said nothing. He agreed with Blake in one sense. The dog caused far too much of a ruckus in the wagon train, but they both knew that ever since Mrs. Kane lost her young daughter in a twister a few weeks earlier, she'd mourned terribly. Finding the half-wolf puppy shivering and abandoned on the plains had filled a void in her heart and started a process of healing the jagged tear left by the death of her only child. "I'll keep an eye on the pup."

"See that you do, or I'll have Zach take him out and shoot him." The tension in Blake's voice raised Sam's concern. It wasn't like him to be this insistent over something so petty, even when facing danger from natives. Blake had fought in as many battles as Sam himself, and Sam had never known his friend to face danger with less than the steadiest of nerves.

"Somethin' troubling you besides the Cheyenne, Blake?"

The wagon master kept his gaze focused on the western horizon, even though the darkness obscured any view. His jaw clenched.

Whatever it was, his friend needed coaxing to share. And Sam didn't coax. He figured a man had a right to his own thoughts and unless he chose to open up, it was no one else's business what was going on in his head.

Blake breathed another heavy sigh. "I wish we could go around the fort."

"We can." Sam looked at him askance. "You're in charge."

Pursing his lips, Blake appeared to consider the thought for a minute. He shook his head. "No. Folks haven't had a break from the trail in too many weeks. And two of Captain Randall's hunters came back with two antelope. They've been roasting them. The scouts have told us the women at the fort are preparing for a real feast tomorrow when we arrive."

Again, Sam kept silent. And Blake continued. "Maybe a diversion'll stop the petty arguments we've been having to put up with. That Kane puppy is just one issue lately. There's the squalling Jenkins baby that keeps everyone within ten wagons either way awake half the night, the heat is getting to everyone, and the thought of climbing the mountains soon has the whole company nervous. Not to mention those pesky redskins."

Sam nodded. "I was thinking of holding a prayer service before we move on from Fort Laramie. You have a problem with that idea?"

Blake gave his hat a two-fingered shove and swiped the sweat from his brow with the back of his arm. "Might not be a bad idea. We'll need all the extra help from above we can get."

A barking flash of black and gray fur tore out past them. Blake let up a growl. "Especially if Kane doesn't do something about that dadblamed dog."

Two

Weary and travel-worn, the pioneers slowly rolled toward the fort. Everyone breathed a little easier when the soldiers appeared at midday to escort them the rest of the way. In the absence of any further threat from the Cheyenne, spirits were beginning to lift and Blake had allowed for walking alongside the wagons. As long as no one drifted off.

Toni would have loved nothing more than to climb down from the narrow wagon seat and stretch her legs, but she didn't dare take the time. She grappled for her shears, as the oxen jerked to the side, tossing her hard on the seat. She held on as the wagon dipped and swayed in the deep ruts of the well-worn trail, making it awfully difficult for Toni to sew a straight line. Some might call her crazy for even attempting such a feat under these harsh conditions. But she was determined to finish Fannie's wedding gown before they reached the fort.

"Is Blake sure there's a preacher at the fort?" she asked.

On the wagon seat next to her, Fannie gripped the reins

in a white-knuckle hold, fighting the lumbering team of oxen as they struggled to keep their footing. "That's what he said." She gave her a quick glance and rolled her eyes. "Apparently that information was part of the scouting expedition."

The first burst of laughter in days made its way through Toni's throat. "He certainly isn't a man to be deterred from his goal, is he?"

"Just like you." She nodded to the gown. "I don't know how on earth you're making such lovely stitches with the wagon moving so much."

Pleased with the compliment, Toni smiled at her friend. "If you're determined to marry Blake before we reach Oregon, then I'm determined you will not do so in those dusty trousers you insist upon wearing."

"There's always the blue gown Edna cut down for me."

"Ah, yes, the night the last group of starry-eyed couples got married. Still, I don't think you want to get married in a hand-me-down, do you?"

Fannie wrinkled her freckled nose. "Not really."

"Well, then. My task is all too clear." Toni sent her an affectionate smile. "Sam said we'll be circling the wagons within the next three hours. If I know your stubborn Mr. Tanner, he'll be hauling you off toward the fort before the oxen are unhitched. So stop distracting me."

"So-rry, Lady." Fannie swatted at the oxen with the reins, and laughed almost a giddy sort of laugh. The joy in Fannie's voice left an ache of gratitude in Toni's heart. Fannie deserved all the happiness life could bring her. Thank God Fannie had escaped Tom before he had broken her spirit.

The way George and every other man who had ever abused Toni had finally beaten her down.

Toni knew she'd had a close call with that last beating. George had truly almost killed her. But never again. He was out of her life for good. Blake and Sam . . . and God . . . had seen to that.

And after all these years of entertaining men so that George could line his pockets, she had finally won. Yes. She, Toni Rodden, had finally won for the first time in her twenty-two years—or at least for the first time in the last seven years since she'd foolishly believed a man and left the safety of her pa's house.

She mopped at her sweat-soaked neck and wished like the dickens an errant cloud would cover the sun, if only for five minutes. A little relief from the torturous heat. Even a soaking cloud burst would be more than welcome.

On miserable days, such as this one, it was difficult for the travelers to remember that summer heat would soon give way to autumn. Then things would cool down probably more than they wished for considering how many times the train had been delayed. According to Sam and Blake, there was some concern about the train's ability to get through the mountains before the snows became too heavy.

But in heat as sweltering as this, most folks weren't looking that far ahead. For now tempers were as short as the days were long and it didn't take much to set anyone off. Feuds sprang up left and right, the most notable among them between Zach Kane and Curtis Adams—all because of a dead chicken.

Lucille, Curtis's wife, swore up and down that Zach's half-wolf pup had killed the fowl and Curtis had no reason to disbelieve his wife. The two men had come close to a duel before Blake put a stop to the foolishness. The travelers, in desperate need of a distraction, had begun to take sides. A dead chicken and a naughty pup had split a 250-member wagon train down the middle. Toni had to shake her head at the nonsense, although secretly she figured *pups will be pups, keep the chickens in a pen and they won't be eaten until you're ready to eat them yourself.* Still, such foolishness to allow a couple of animals to cause this much emotional upheaval.

Thankfully, for today, an unspoken truce remained in effect. Folks had other things on their minds. The Indians. And Fort Laramie, for instance. Even yesterday's threat couldn't dampen their spirits for the wonderful distraction that lay just ahead. And beyond that, the mountains, and beyond that . . . Oregon. The promised land.

Before leaving Hawkins, Kansas, Toni had imagined that land of milk and honey as her new beginning. A husband. Children. All the things a woman held in her heart from childhood. Although most scoffed at the notion of a "soiled dove" attracting any man willing to spend more than a few hours in her bed, let alone a lifetime with her, she had held out hope. Cautiously, but hope nonetheless.

But now that her beauty was marred, she'd forever buried those romantic notions. If she didn't have her beauty, what would she have to offer? Not enough to cover up her past. Her current ambitions hinged on two things: her skills as a seamstress and the short memories of her fellow travelers.

Now that she was no longer a threat for their husbands' attention, she hoped the women of the train would begin to extend mercy and not always sweep aside their skirts when they saw her coming.

Eventually, she wanted to own a little dress shop. Until then, she could mend tears and make shirts for men who were without wives or mothers to sew for them. But none of that would happen if she couldn't make a fresh start in folks' minds.

Toni sewed the last stitch of Fannie's wedding gown moments before the walls of Fort Laramie became the left flank of the wagon train and the order filtered down the line, "Circle the wagons!"

"Here comes Two-Feathers." Fannie's words brought Toni's head up just as she snipped the loose thread with a relieved sigh. She smiled a welcome to the sinewy scout. In spite of herself, Toni never failed to marvel at the sight of Sam astride his horse. If ever a more handsome man existed, she had yet to meet him. And she'd known more men than she cared to count.

"The Captain has invited all the ladies to sleep in the barracks tonight."

Toni's eyes narrowed. "Why would we want to do that?"

Sam's brow creased into a frown, then his hazel eyes shone with understanding. "He thought you might enjoy sleeping indoors on army cots instead of on the ground or inside the wagon on a pallet."

Heat seared Toni's cheeks. Of course the offer wasn't meant as a proposition of any kind. What must Sam think of her for even imagining such a thing? Still, wouldn't anyone with her past naturally be suspicious of any man who offered her his bed? In her experience, most men would have been in the bed as well.

"You don't have to do it," Sam assured her in his soft, gentle tone. "Many women will choose to remain with their husbands."

"What about the children?" Fannie asked, her voice tight and wrought with irritation. "Or are the women to leave them behind for their men to look after?

Toni had noticed over the last few miles that Fannie's temper had grown shorter. She expected the new-bride giddiness was beginning to give way to wedding-night jitters. She didn't blame her. Fannie's experience with men had been limited to an enormous pig of a man with bad breath and cruel intentions. But hopefully, the love of a truly good man—and Blake was that, even if he didn't have any use for Toni—would show Fannie that the bed of marriage was different. Marriage was no guarantee, but she prayed it would be so for Fannie.

Poor Sam blinked and seemed at a loss for words. Toni was sure he hadn't expected to be faced with a suspicious ex-prostitute and a jittery bride-to-be. They could have been a little more gracious, she supposed.

"Are the mothers to bring their children with them, Sam?" Toni urged.

He nodded, apparent relief swathing his chiseled features. "All girls may accompany their mothers, also the boys under the age of six."

That sounded logical. Most of the rough-and-tumble camp boys would have howled with dismay at the very thought of being banished to quarters with the women. Still, she seriously doubted many of the mothers of such small boys would leave them to the mercy of their fathers.

Toni smoothed the fabric on her lap and cleared her throat. If they were going to have time for Fannie to try on the gown before dinner, they'd best get a move on with chores. "Thank you for letting us know, Sam."

"May I escort you into the fort when you're ready, Miss Toni?"

The offer came as a surprise to Toni. A welcome surprise. Maybe she hadn't realized until this moment how nervous she was at the thought of walking into a fort filled with soldiers, many of whom hadn't held a woman for a long time. Not that she expected much attention, but the thought made her nervous.

"That would be lovely, Sam." She smiled and wondered at his deepening complexion. *Was that a blush? No. It couldn't be.* She dismissed the thought as he tipped his hat and rode away, sitting straight, almost regal, in the saddle.

Weeks ago, Sam had made it abundantly clear that he had no right to think romantically of a woman like her. She understood. A former prostitute and a man of God like Sam. It would never work. He'd surely never see her as anything more than a woman in need of redemption.

"Unless I miss my bet, you might be making your own wedding gown before long," Fannie said with a nudge as she maneuvered the oxen into place.

"Wedding?" Toni couldn't hide the shock in her voice. "You know better than that. You were sitting right next to me when I told you how Sam felt."

"You mean . . . about not having any right to think of you that way?"

"Exactly. A man like that isn't going to look twice at a prostitute. Even if I wanted him to."

"Former prostitute," Fannie corrected. "You're not the same as you used to be. You're a Christian now, you read your Bible and everything. If what Sam said is true, that past is gone and as far as God is concerned you're as innocent as a newborn babe. And Sam's got no right to hold your past against you." Fannie's voice rose as it did when her hot temper got the better of her.

Toni appreciated the support, but this time no amount of anger or indignation could change the truth that was stacked against Toni's future with a man as kind and good as Sam.

"That might be true. But Sam's not God." Toni absently wrapped her hair around her finger then pulled it across her cheek. She really had tried to wear it up as Blake had suggested might be more fitting, but it was impossible to hide the scars with her hair pinned.

"Let me put your hair up for you tonight," Fannie suggested.

Toni shook her head and fingered the raised scars. "I'd rather leave it down."

"I understand." Fannie climbed down as her younger brother Kip rode his horse toward their wagon, his eyes bright and eager. "Blake said I can go to the fort as soon as I get the team unhitched and fed."

A frown creased Fannie's brow. "He did? Without discussing it with me?"

The boy gave a deep scowl. "I ain't a baby."

"Maybe not," Fannie said with firm resolve. "But no one has the right to tell you where you can and can't go except for me. Not even Blake." Fannie's nerves, being on edge the way they were, obviously could take no more unexpected surprises—good or bad. Blake should have known better. The girl was getting into a lather over the situation.

Toni climbed down from the wagon and looked directly at the boy. "What exactly did Blake say, Kip?"

Rolling his eyes, he went to work on the leather straps. "Oh, well, he said Fannie has to say it's okay."

"See, Fannie? Blake wasn't trying to take over with Kip. Just relax." Toni gave her a playful shove. "Now hurry and finish up your chores so we can get you ready."

A crooked grin tugged at Fannie's lips as she realized she had nearly blown up at Blake for nothing. "All right. I'll go gather up buffalo chips with the children. It won't take long."

"I'll have water ready for you to wash."

Kip began unhitching the team. "Blake said to tell you the women are excused from camp chores except for personal fires and animals. Since we're eating at the fort." He jerked his thumb in the direction of a wooded area on the other side of the train from where the fort sat. "There's a lake over yonder. It's not far, but no one can go alone. And at least one person has to carry a gun."

A happy bubble rose inside of Toni. "Are we allowed to bathe?"

The twelve-year-old boy shrugged, too busy working on his chore to worry about such frivolous thoughts. He finished unyoking the beautiful red beasts and slapped them on the rump, sending them off to the center of the circle where they would be free to graze.

"I'll find out," Fannie said swiftly. "I'm taking your horse."

"Careful not to spook him," Kip warned. "He's jumpy from all the excitement."

She rolled her eyes. "If you can handle him, I can."

Toni had no doubt her little friend was right. Fannie had endured more in her eighteen years than most women endured in a lifetime. She was grateful at least that the girl had only had to endure the abuses of one man. Toni, on the other hand, wasn't able to look at a man without wondering how he intended to harm her. Every man except for Sam Two-Feathers.

Dusk was beginning to fall and Sam's stomach grumbled as the heady aroma of antelope roasting over slow-burning fires reached his nose in a most pleasing fashion. He figured Toni had been ready to go over an hour ago. Only he'd been delayed by one thing or another and was forced to keep her waiting.

He'd already seen Fannie and Blake, accompanied by little Katie, wander hand in hand toward the wooden structure. In fact, the camp was more bare than he'd seen it since the train had set out. Except for the guards, who had been tripled just in case the Cheyenne returned, very few people remained in camp. Although there had been no signs of the Indians, Blake still didn't want to take any chances. And Sam agreed one hundred percent.

He could kick himself for being so late. Toni must think he'd forgotten her, but in Blake's absence, it was up to Sam to make sure the wagon train was secure. He'd been forced to resolve the latest skirmish between two of the young men vying for the attention of pretty Ruth Shewmate, who was traveling with her brother and his new wife. The whole train, Mrs. Shewmate especially, Sam suspected, hoped Ruth would make up her mind soon and marry one of the poor saps.

As late as he was, Sam feared Toni might have gone on to the fort without him, and he wouldn't be offended if she had. Still, he couldn't help but be gratified when he reached the wagon and found her sitting on the wagon tongue staring pensively into the woods rather than in the direction of the fort.

Before he could apologize, she glanced up and smiled. "You didn't back out after all, I see."

"Why would I do that?"

She gave a shrug and returned her attention to the sunset. "I just thought you might."

"Only a fool would give up the chance to escort the prettiest woman in the wagon train."

Without suffering him a glance she gave a humorless laugh. "You don't have to flatter me, Sam."

"You're very lovely, Miss Toni. But even more important than your outward appearance, you have an inward beauty. When I say you're the most beautiful woman in the train, I mean it. In all ways, you're a woman worthy of praise."

She smiled. "Because I fear the Lord?"

Pleased, Sam smiled back and nodded. "You've been reading your Bible."

"Yes." She gave a little laugh. "Although I'm not fully convinced the woman described in Proverbs 31 was a real woman. If she was, I'd love to meet her and ask her the secret to having it all."

"Perhaps you will meet her in heaven one day—if she was indeed a real woman."

"Perhaps."

"What was your mother like, Sam?" Toni asked, tilting her head slightly to look up at him.

Sam tensed. He wasn't one to think about his childhood and his mother had died before his fifteenth birthday. From childhood in the Sioux village, he'd always known he wasn't like the rest. His light skin had caused years of ridicule from the other boys. He'd never felt he fit. In the Indian world or the white world.

"It's all right, Sam," she said softly. "You don't have to talk about her if you don't want to."

But as Sam searched Toni's earnest face, he knew he could trust her with his past, just as she could trust him with hers.

"My mother was a Dakota Sioux."

"So your pa was white?"

Sam gave a solemn nod, fighting the constant battle with anger that rose up inside of his chest each time he thought of the man who had fathered him.

"Where are they now?" Toni gently prodded.

"I do not know whether my father lives or not. My mother died many years ago."

Toni reached out and placed her hand on his arm. The subtle gesture tugged at his heart. He covered her hand with his own. Only for a second. "How did they meet?" she asked.

"My father was a fur trader and came to the village to trade. My mother was a young woman, ready for marriage. They were married according to the Sioux customs and she went with him. A few months later, he was ready to leave the mountains and return to his home in Kansas. He told her he couldn't take her with him because he had a white wife and family waiting for him. My mother returned home in disgrace. But her people welcomed her back and a few months later, I was born."

"The poor woman." Toni's face gentled with compassion.

"When I was ten years old, she took me and went looking for my father, the man she loved."

"Did she find him?"

Sam shook his head. "A lone woman with a boy? She didn't know where he was. It was foolish of her to even try. But her heart would not allow her to remain."

"Did she return home?"

"No. We wandered many weeks until finally, we came to a ranch in Missouri. The people were kind and gave mother a position washing clothes and cooking meals. This is where we stayed until my mother died. I worked as a ranch hand almost from the first day we arrived."

"When you were ten years old?" Toni's incredulous tone made him smile. "That's ridiculous."

"It was a good thing. The head ranch hand taught me many things about taking care of horses and identifying animals according to their tracks or droppings. He taught me the things a father should have. Because of his training, I was ready to be a tracker by the time I left at fifteen."

"How did your mother die?"

Sadness clutched Sam's heart. "Childbirth. She fell in love with one of the ranch hands and they married a year after we arrived at the ranch. Her husband, Sol, was a good man. He loved my mother and treated her well."

"I'm glad."

"Before she died, she asked me to go back to her people and tell my grandfather of her death. And that's what I did."

"Did you ever return to the ranch?"

Sam shook his head. "I found the wagon train and hired on as a tracker."

He had lived with the Sioux for a year, learning their ways and sharing Jesus with them. In the end, he had made several converts, but most wanted nothing to do with the gospel.

"So you've haven't had a home since you left with your mother as a boy?"

A smile tipped Sam's lips. "My home is in heaven. While I'm on earth my home is wherever God tells me to go. Right now, I'm living the life I'm supposed to live."

"But don't you want a family?" Toni's voice softened and she averted her gaze.

"Yes. I pray that God will send me a wife. I'd love nothing more than to settle down and build a life with someone."

"That would be nice." Toni gave him a tiny smile. "A good man like you deserves to be happily married with a passel of children."

The image that rose from her words included Toni herself, and the passel of children looked just like her.

Silence loomed between them until Sam sensed a change of conversation was in order. Which was fine with him. He was ready to proudly escort this enchanting woman to the fort and share a meal and perhaps a dance with her. "Are you ready to accompany me to the fort?"

A cloud shadowed her face and Sam knew what was coming.

"Sam, would you mind if I change my mind and stay away from the celebration tonight?" She shuddered a little. "I know I said I would go, but I'd truly rather not."

Disappointment shuffled through him. But he knew better than to try to hold on to something that didn't want to be held. "You are free to choose, Miss Toni."

She reached forward and touched his hand. "Thank you, Sam. I think I'd rather stay here and enjoy the beautiful night sky. It's so peaceful with most of the camp inside the fort." She gave another short laugh, this time with a twinkle in her eyes. "The way these people like to feud, peace is a rare commodity I'd like to take full advantage of."

Sam couldn't say he blamed her; still, he felt the disappointment down to his moccasins that she hadn't invited him to enjoy the peaceful evening with her.

Hesitating only a second just in case she changed her mind, he hung back, then gave a nod as it became evident by her quiet perusal of the night sky that she would prefer to be alone. "Very well, I'll leave you to your own thoughts."

"Thank you." She smiled. "Have a wonderful time at the celebration."

"Be sure not to walk away from camp, Miss Toni." Sam searched her face to make sure she truly did understand that he meant what he said.

"I'll be fine, Sam."

That wasn't exactly the reassurance he'd hoped for, but he supposed he'd have to let it go. Besides, she truly did appear to seek solitude.

"Goodnight then. Enjoy your evening."

As he walked away, Sam had to fight to keep from turning back and planting himself right next to Toni on the ground, sharing the wagon wheel as a backrest. He would have liked nothing more than to enjoy this lovely sunset and the coming moon with Toni. As a matter of fact, nothing would have pleased him more, but Sam recognized Toni's plea for what it was. She desperately needed to be alone with her thoughts. He only prayed that some of those thoughts veered favorably in his direction.

Three

Ginger Freeman wasn't exactly the type of person to hold a grudge. When James Walker dipped her ribbons in the inkwell during her school days, she never told the teacher, and even suffered a trip to the woodshed when she took the blame and told Pa she had lost them swimming in the river. When Zoe Barker called her dirty and stupid, she quickly forgave the girl, even shared her pa's fried chicken. She forgave her ma for running off with that man when Ginger was only thirteen years old and needed a mother most. In short, she'd had a lot of practice letting go of anger. But no longer.

As she searched among the pioneers, anger burned her heart. So far none of the laughing, frolicking, dancing settlers held any resemblance to the man she remembered from seven years ago. She'd only been eleven years old, but the vision of his uncaring eyes was branded into her memory forever. He was tall, with brown hair, brown eyes. Nondescript by a lot of standards. Still, Ginger hadn't traveled from

Missouri, following the man's trail, just to walk away empty-handed.

Frustration threatened to burn up her insides as she realized she wasn't going to find him. She fingered the Colt hanging from her hip and glanced at the gate again. He must have stayed in camp. That was the only explanation.

"May I have this dance, miss?"

Ginger scowled up at a red-faced youth of no more than sixteen who stood in front of her, grinning a stupid grin that spread across his entire face. "Leave me alone," she snapped. "Do I look like I'm in the mood to dance?"

"Y-yes, miss, I-I mean no," he squeaked, going redder than before. "Sorry."

"Little fool," she muttered and continued toward the gate. The guard, a private with a rifle slung across one shoulder, stopped her before she could slip outside.

"I can't let you outside the fort alone, miss."

Ginger met his gaze with a steady frown. "I can take care of myself. And I got to get back to camp."

"You-uh, you're part of the wagon train?"

Relief filled her that he believed her so readily. The fort wasn't that large, but she hadn't been here very long, and she'd kept to herself for the most part, so he obviously didn't recognize her. "That's right. My baby is sick and I need to get back to camp and take care of him."

A frown creased his brow. "You left your sick baby?"

"Well, I couldn't very well bring it to the fort, could I?" This fella didn't have a lick of sense she had detected so far.

"I don't suppose . . ."

Sending him a fierce look of disdain, Ginger took a step toward the gate. "Now let me out so I can go take care of my son."

The guard scratched his head beneath his cap. He hesitated.

"Do I need to call the wagon master? Or perhaps your captain?"

"I don't know. I was told no unaccompanied women were allowed through the gate."

Noting the chink in his armor, Ginger pounced while he was undecided. She stepped closer and shoved her finger against his chest. "If my baby dies, you're the one I'm coming after, soldier. Do you want her death on your hands?"

"Her? I thought you said it was a boy."

Swallowing hard, Ginger forced a sarcastic little laugh. Thank mercy that soldier had more brawn than sense. It shouldn't take too much to convince him. "No. Little Sarah is definitely a girl."

"But I could have sworn . . ."

"You calling me a liar?"

Alarm shot to his eyes. "No, miss—er—ma'am."

"Then move aside and let me out of this confounded fort. I vow, I'll never set foot inside here again if I'm to be treated like a prisoner!"

"May I arrange for an escort for you? Your husband, perhaps?"

"Husband? Who said anything about a husband?" Oh! Ginger's face burned and she was thankful for the cover of darkness to hide what was surely a blush.

"You don't have a husband, ma'am—er—miss?"

"For heaven's sake of course I have a husband. What sort of woman do you take me for?"

"Well, I'm sorry, I didn't mean to imply . . ."

"Perhaps you should think twice before you accuse a woman of not having a husband! I've never been more insulted in my life. Now get out of my way before I report your behavior to your superiors."

He stumbled backward, swallowing so hard his Adam's apple bobbed up and down in his throat. "Yes, ma'am. I apologize for my unforgivable rudeness to a l-lady."

Ginger decided to ignore the way he stumbled over calling her a lady. After all, she couldn't blame him. Considering the way she was dressed and the lie he must surely be wise to. Still, in the absence of proof, he had no choice but to let her go or suffer consequences should she be telling the truth. In short, Ginger had him over a barrel. And they both knew it.

Toni leaned back, allowing the breeze to blow across her hair, neck, face. She wished fervently it was a cooling breeze, but even at dusk, the heat lingered. Not as scorching as a couple of hours ago, but still too hot to truly relax.

Earlier, Blake had allowed for baths in the creek, but Toni hadn't been able to force herself to undress before the women who had judged her every single day during the past months, turning their backs on her and generally making her feel more unclean than the layers of dust covering her body ever could.

Blake had warned the entire train . . . women in particular, not to leave the camp without a companion and a gun. For any reason. As if they hadn't already figured out the obvious, Blake couldn't have stressed enough that the Cheyenne Indians in these parts were notorious for causing trouble for wagon trains. Venturing out alone was strictly forbidden. And once again, all eyes had swung to Toni. Would there ever come a day when she didn't feel personally responsible for any trouble facing the wagon train?

At the moment, she had neither companion nor gun. Only a burning desire to dip in the water and find relief from the unrelenting heat. Besides, there had been no sign of the Indians since the day before. Toni couldn't imagine anyone wanting her enough to start a war.

The more Toni sat in the sweltering heat, listening to the music and laughter coming from the fort, the more isolated she felt. She chafed at the confinement. Who would know if she dipped into the water and then returned before the rest of the wagon train. Why should they get to enjoy themselves while she sat in the miserable heat? And she really did need to bathe. She was beginning to offend herself so she could only imagine how bad she smelled to others. Especially now that most of the women of the train had taken the opportunity to wash off the trail dust and grime. And what if Fannie did come back from the fort with the news of her impending wedding? Toni wouldn't have another opportunity to bathe before the ceremony. And she'd be darned if she was going to attend her friend's wedding in a filthy dress covering an equally filthy body. Besides, she could be there and back before anyone was the wiser. After all, the music had barely begun.

It didn't take a minute for her to come to a decision. She shot to her feet and ducked inside the wagon, grabbing soap, brush, linen to dry herself with. She bundled her second dress and a fresh petticoat and backed out of the canvas.

By the light of the bright moon, she made her way the mile and a half to where the lake rippled peacefully beneath the starlit sky. This was more like it. She sat on the bank and began unhooking her boots. She removed one, then the other, sighing in relief and wiggling her stockinged toes. But that was nowhere near good enough. Standing, she began the task of unbuttoning her dress. In moments, she had stripped down to her petticoat and bare feet.

The air caressed her bare arms and a smile reached her lips as the heat of the day dissipated into the coolness of the gentle breeze blowing off the water.

She toed the water. Cool, inviting, refreshing. Unable to resist for one more second, Toni waded in, grateful that her pa had insisted she learn to swim before her sixth birthday. Pebbles massaged her feet as she walked deeper and deeper into the soothing waters.

Before long, only her neck and head remained dry. In the caress of the gentle current, all thoughts of dangerous animals and Indians fled her mind. She cupped her hands and gathered the water as her body became one with the lake. For the first time in years, Toni moved without fear, without self-consciousness. The water felt so refreshingly simple, her frustrations melted and peace flooded her heart. On a whim, she turned over and floated on her back, staring at the sky and imagining God in his glory looking down upon her. "Do you see me?" she whispered into the darkness. "Am I really clean like Sam claims I am?"

Tears pricked her eyes. She knew the words Sam had spoken. Knew in her head that the Bible indeed stated that she was a new creature. That all of her past was behind her. That she would never be that woman she used to be.

So why didn't she feel new? Some days she did. Sometimes, especially when she read the Bible by firelight or listened to Sam's preaching over the campfire for anyone who cared to join the Bible reading. But other times . . . images assaulted her, making her feel violated all over again. No matter how she fought against it, in her mind's eye, she saw them. The men. She couldn't remember names, but no matter how hard she prayed, those faces stayed with her.

She closed her eyes and sank under the water. Perhaps it would be easier if she allowed the deep to consume her, forever silencing the menacing, mocking voices insisting that she was no good.

Grant Kelley moved stealthily through the darkness, wishing the moon wasn't quite so bright. He knew he was being followed. Had even spotted his pursuer in a quick movement. The small figure clad in buckskin certainly wasn't very skilled in keeping quiet. Every footfall sounded like a buffalo stampede.

He'd known from the minute he followed Toni from camp, that he, too, was being followed. The only thing he couldn't figure out was why.

Nor could he figure out why Toni had been foolish enough to defy Blake's orders and leave the campsite alone. After their close call with the Cheyenne the day before, she, better than anyone, should understand that the threat of an Indian attack was as real as Blake had indicated. Grant himself had seen further signs of the natives, though he hadn't shared the information just yet. There had been no opportunity. Nevertheless, the person following was no Indian and Grant was tired of the game.

He was just about to whip around and confront his poorly concealed tracker when a scream filled the air.

"What was that?" a woman's voice called behind him. Figures the stalker wasn't even a man, but a woman. That explained a few things.

"You know as much as I do," he shouted back and took off at a run in the direction of the lake.

Sam's heart nearly burst from his chest at the sound of Toni's cry. He stayed hidden and assessed the situation. Satisfied that there were no hostiles threatening her, he stepped out of the woods. "Miss Toni?" he called softly. "Is something wrong?"

"Sam?" she hissed from the water, "Is that you?"

Her tone was a mixture of fear and relief.

"It is me."

"I-I feel foolish." She moved through the water, heading

toward the bank where he stood. Sam swallowed hard, using every bit of will and a heartfelt prayer heavenward to find the strength to avert his gaze. The sound of Toni's nervous laughter put him at ease to the reality that she was in no danger. He turned his back while she exited the creek.

"A snake swam across my legs."

Sam's lips twisted into a smile. "You have nothing to feel foolish about."

She snorted. "I bet no Indian woman would be afraid of a little snake."

"Perhaps she wouldn't let out a scream, but I suspect there are not too many women, Indian or white, who would not cringe as a snake slithered across their legs."

"Thanks, Sam. I'm not sure I feel much better. But at least you tried." She gave a laugh. "You can turn around now. I'm dressed."

Sam slowly inched around. "You're still trembling."

She nodded. A sob tore at her throat and instantly Sam moved forward, taking the slight form in his arms. She clung to him without resistance. That alone tugged at his heart as much as the sobs. He held her firmly, but gently, one arm around her waist, the other caressing her wet hair that hung down her back. The smell of the lake clung to her and the earthy scent of a summer wind nearly clouded his senses. It was all he could do not to give in to the temptation to kiss away her fears. It wouldn't take much. Just a small shift, a kiss on the cheek, one closer to her lips, and if she didn't pull away, he could claim her lips. Sam's heart nearly pounded from his chest as he wove his fingers through her thick hair.

Her soft sigh was all the encouragement he needed. "Toni," he whispered.

The sound of footsteps crashed into the clearing, jolting Sam from his thoughts and instantly bringing him to his senses. Sam turned just in time to see Grant Kelley, followed closely by someone he had never seen before. Grant made a grab for the stranger, but it was too late as the moon glowed across the barrel of a Colt revolver.

"Turn her loose, mister," came the command in a distinctly feminine voice. "And I mean now."

Toni gasped as Sam dropped his arms from her waist and went for his gun.

"I wouldn't if I was you!" the woman warned.

"Who are you?" Sam asked, his voice cold as steel.

"I'm the person that's going to plug you full of lead if you don't move away from her." She nodded at Toni. "You okay?"

"Of course I am. Sam wouldn't hurt me in a million years."

"He's not trying anything with you?"

"Oh, for mercy's sake. What gave you that idea?"

"What do you think? You screamed like a banshee."

Toni let out a laugh that Sam suspected was more from nerves than amusement. "I suppose I did. But honestly, a snake spooked me, that's all."

"Then what's he doing here?" The girl gave a pointed nod toward Sam. "He your husband?"

"I don't have a husband." Sam swallowed hard as Toni's frown revealed her own thoughts before she spoke, "She has a point, Sam. What were you doing out here?"

There was no disguising his actions. If only she would believe his motives. "I saw you leave camp and followed to make sure you remained safe."

"You . . . watched me?" The dismay in her voice touched a tender place in Sam's heart reserved only for her. "Not like you're thinking," he said softly. "You have my word. I averted my eyes as you disrobed and entered the water."

The young woman holding the gun let out a snort. Toni turned on her. "Put that thing away," she commanded. "As you can see, no one is in any danger here. At least not from Sam."

"I reckon that settles it then." The woman holstered her pistol. "I guess you two have everything under control."

Sam bristled at the suggestion in her tone. He stepped forward. Toni placed a restraining hand on his arm. "Don't, Sam. I have no reputation to protect."

"I think we'd better get back to camp," Grant Kelley spoke for the first time. He took hold of the woman's arm. "And you can explain why you were following me in the first place."

Sam's mind raced back over Toni's words as he watched Grant half-lead, half-drag the buckskin-wearing woman toward camp. Toni followed, only the tiniest slump in her shoulders indicating that she felt the woman's insinuation to the core.

Lord, what can I do or say to help her believe that You don't hold her past against her?

Four

Toni said a hasty goodnight to Sam and crawled wearily into her pallet at the edge of the wagon. She'd been forced to sleep inside since the incident with the Indian. And that meant suffering the sweltering heat inside the wagon instead of under it, which she preferred. She was determined to procure a tent from someone inside the fort before they rolled westward again.

She and Fannie had agreed they would not take the Captain up on his offer of a cot in the officers' quarters. They preferred the bottom of a wagon to the whispers, stares, and deliberate snubs from the other women. Not all, of course. Sadie Barnes; Edna Stewart, who had once held out hope that Blake would marry her; and Mrs. James, whose husband had been forced to leave the wagon train after he'd thrown his lot in with the men aiming to take Toni and Fannie captive; these women treated Fannie and Toni well. A few of the other women suffered their presence, but the two friends had agreed they preferred to stick together.

The gentle breeze carried the distant strains of "I'll Take you Home Again, Kathleen" from the fort. Toni closed her eyes and imagined the dancing couples holding each other. Enjoying their respite. Unbidden, her mind reached back to the too-brief moment when Sam's arms cradled her as she wept. But there was no point in dwelling on what might have been. Especially when her curiosity rose at the thought of the young woman clad in buckskins.

She wondered about the new young woman. Even though she had barreled in and interrupted a private moment, it was difficult to be angry with someone who would have come to her rescue and would have been most welcome had the threat been real.

Still, Grant Kelley, one of the captains of the train who served as a scout alongside Sam, hadn't seemed a bit impressed with her bravery. It dawned on Toni (she had been so wrapped up in her own dilemma) that she'd never even asked the girl her name or thanked her for her rescue attempt.

Sam looked from Grant to the young woman dressed like a man. The battle of wills between these two would have been comical if not for the questions roaming through Sam's mind. In Blake's absence, he had a decision to make. Only, he wasn't sure exactly what that decision consisted of.

"What is your name?" he asked. "And state the reason that you defied the Captain's orders and ventured out to our camp." Blake and the Captain had agreed at the fort that no one from the fort was allowed in their camp after nightfall.

And here this woman had disobeyed that directive the very first night.

"Ginger," she practically spat out. "That's my name."

"Ginger what?"

"That's my business."

Sam nodded. "Fair enough. And your purpose for coming into camp?"

"I didn't." She gave him a frank stare. "I was headed to the creek for a bath—I like to bathe alone at night—when I saw the woman leave and this man follow her."

Jealousy hit Sam. Unbidden and certainly unwanted. Why would Grant follow Toni? He turned to the man with whom he had spent the last few months working side by side. "Grant?"

"If I'd known you were looking out for Toni I wouldn't have bothered. But you know you don't make a sound or leave a trail so it wasn't obvious."

"Why not just stop her from leaving camp in the first place?" Ginger said, suspicion written all over her features— which were pleasant enough—but not as beautiful as Toni, by any stretch of the imagination. Her hair was dark. Not black, but a deep brown. Even in the light of the campfire, he noted her eyes were about as dark as her hair. If her features had been more pronounced, he might have guessed her to be part Indian. He turned to Grant for the answer to Ginger's question.

"Not that I owe you an explanation," Grant said, scowling deeply at the young woman. He turned back to Sam. "I heard some of the women talking earlier." He cleared his throat and darted a glance to Ginger, whose arms were folded across her chest. "It seems Toni didn't bathe when the other women did. They seemed to be gossiping. You know how women do." Annoyance slid across his face. "I figured she didn't want to undress in front of them and waited until everyone was gone for some privacy. Stopping her didn't seem right. So I followed her to keep an eye on her. But I thought it would be better to stay out of sight."

"Of all the cockamamie stories." Ginger stomped her foot and jabbed a finger toward Grant. "Are you going to believe that hogwash?"

A quick perusal of the situation brought a swift decision. "Yes. I have no reason to call this man a liar."

"Thank you, Sam," Grant said with a nod of acceptance. "I appreciate the confidence."

"Fine. If you'll excuse me. I'm going back to the fort."

"Not by yourself, you're not," Grant said.

"Who's going to stop me?"

"I'm not stopping you, but I'm not letting you go alone either."

Anger flashed in the woman's eyes. "You seem to make a habit of following women who'd rather be alone."

Sam tried not to grin. It really wasn't fair to Grant considering he'd only been trying to protect Toni, just as he was bent on protecting this young woman. But he'd never seen a woman put Grant in his place before.

From the fort, the sound of the bugle announced the end of the day.

"I'm afraid it's too late for you to return to the fort to-night," Sam said.

The young woman frowned. "What do you mean? You're keeping me here against my will?"

"No, miss," Sam replied. "The reveille has sounded. The last of our people will be on their way back and the gate closed and locked for the night. They will not open the gate for you."

His words seemed to silence her and she frowned as though in heavy thought. Expelling a breath, she planted her hands on her hips. "First they won't let me out, now they won't let me in." She gave Sam a pointed stare. "Where's a lady supposed to sleep?"

Sam made a quick decision. "Grant, will you please escort Miss Ginger to Miss Sadie's tent and ask if she'd be willing to put this woman up for the night?"

Sam watched them go, pleased with himself. This solved two problems. It kept the girl from trying to leave camp and got her out of his hair. But he'd be glad to hand her back to the soldiers at the fort first thing in the morning. He had a feeling about this girl and it wasn't necessarily a good one.

Sleep eluded Toni. As much as she tried to force herself to relax, she knew it was futile until Fannie returned with news. Was she going to marry Blake at the fort? Her mind wandered back over the events of the night, and back to Sam's warm arms and rock hard chest. She allowed herself a few moments of weakness and dreamed of gentle caresses and whispered words of love, then pushed them firmly aside as the camp began to fill up with the travelers returning from the fort.

Finally, a knock outside the wagon alerted her to Fannie's presence. "Toni? Are you awake?"

Toni crawled to the opening in the canvas. "What are you knocking for?"

Fannie pointed to Blake, who held a sleeping child in his arms. "Katie couldn't hold her head up another minute." Fannie gave the child a tender smile. "And you know how soundly she sleeps, so Blake carried her home. Can he come in and lay her down?"

Fingering the top of her nightgown, Toni was suddenly struck with a modesty she hadn't known she possessed. "Just a minute. Let me grab my shawl." She draped the shawl over her shoulders and crossed her arms in front of her chest. "I suppose he can come in now." She held back the canvas flap so the wagon master wouldn't have to struggle to climb up to the canvas and crawl over the back of the wagon. Nevertheless, forced to bend low inside the cramped quarters, he stumbled, but righted himself in time to prevent sending Katie and himself tumbling to the floor.

"That pallet," Toni said, feeling the embarrassment of being this close to a man in their very own quarters. It really wasn't decent. Even *she* knew that. And she hadn't been faced with the situation in months. A thrill rose inside of her at the thought that she never again had to entertain a man's presence.

Blake kept his gaze averted from Toni and carefully lowered Katie to the pallet and then cleared his throat. "Night, Toni. Sorry to bother you."

"No bother."

Fannie, who had remained outside, poked her head in. "I'll be there in a minute," she said to Toni.

Toni nodded and closed the canvas flap in order to give her friend some privacy. She heard the low tones of an intimate conversation and then silence. They must be sharing a goodnight kiss. Toni smiled. And just earlier today, Fannie had been on the verge of calling the whole thing off. Thank goodness the girl had come to her senses. Blake wasn't always the most sensitive of men, but it was clear he loved Fannie a great deal.

A few more minutes passed and finally Fannie returned. "How was the celebration at the fort?" Toni asked, practically pouncing on the chance for conversation with her dearest friend. She couldn't wait to tell Fannie about her swim and Sam rescuing her after the snake swam across her legs.

But one look at Fannie's face and Toni knew her friend needed to talk about something much more important.

"Well?" Toni asked, her patience scarcely allowing for Fannie to change into her bed clothes. Fannie's hands trembled as she worked the buttons on the blue dress, but her eyes shone.

"The scouts were right. There's a preacher at the fort."

"Is Blake speaking with him?"

She nodded and slid onto her pallet, lying on top of the covers. "He already did." Taking a quick, deep breath, she lay on her side, head resting in the palm of her hand. "Tomorrow is the day. The Captain said we can hold another dance and he's arranged for Blake and me to have private quarters for the rest of our stopover."

"Fannie, that's wonderful." And it truly was wonderful. Only a twinge of regret pinched Toni's heart now that the plans had indeed been made.

"Blake is purchasing a wagon and team."

"I assumed he would." Toni tried to keep the tremble from her voice.

"Do you know what that means?"

Toni turned on her side, facing Fannie and rested her head in her own palm. "You'll be driving your wagon since Blake has to ride on horseback."

Fannie nodded. "Are you going to be all right driving the wagon alone every day?"

"I'll be fine." But she wasn't sure she would be. There would be no one to take over when she needed to walk, no one to talk to . . . Toni hated things to change. As happy as she was for her friend, she was beginning to see her future for what it was. Alone on the trail, and once they reached Oregon she'd be alone for the rest of her life. She knew Blake would not allow Fannie to be her friend once they arrived at their destination. It would bring too much shame to their home. Tears burned her eyes. She brushed them away quickly.

As though reading her thoughts, Fannie sat up and reached for Toni's hand. "The right man will find his way to you, Toni."

A short laugh escaped Toni's lips. "There is no right man out there for me."

"What about Sam?"

At her friend's words, Toni once again relived the moments of comfort in Sam's arms. But it was useless. "Oh, Fannie. We've discussed this before. Sam's first love is God. A woman like me could never be good enough. He deserves someone . . . better. Pure."

"But . . ."

Toni slid her hand away from Fannie's. "Let's not discuss this. I'd rather talk about tomorrow and how lovely you're going to look in your new wedding gown."

"Oh, Toni. I wish . . ."

"Don't wish, Fannie. I'm resigned to knowing I'll be alone forever."

"Blake says there are several men to every one woman in Oregon. Surely you could find a man."

"Goodness, Fannie. I'd rather be alone than marry a man that settled for me just because he needs a wife."

"I suppose you're right. Still, some women think it's better to have any husband than no husband at all."

"Well, I'm not one of them," Toni replied flatly. "Truly, if I can set up a business for myself and take in sewing for a living, I'll make do just fine." And she truly would. Anything was better than going back to the life she had led. Oh, she knew people thought she'd end up at the first brothel she came to. But they didn't know her. Never again.

Five

The morning of Fannie's wedding arrived dark and overcast, with the worrisome sound of thunder off in the distance.

Toni went about morning chores, boiling coffee, fixing one egg each for Katie, Kip, Fannie, and herself. Plus a stack of flapjacks—a treat she saved only for special occasions and this was special enough to warrant pulling out the jar of honey she and Fannie had been saving. She'd already told Blake and Sam in no uncertain terms that they would have to find their breakfast elsewhere today. Fannie had too much to attend to and couldn't be distracted on her wedding day.

The sky rumbled, as the thunder brought its threat even closer. Toni held her breath for a long second and then breathed out.

Everyone got a little jumpy when storms approached. It was understandable after a spring twister had slammed the wagon train, killing several folks including little Rebecca Kane. The loss of livestock and supplies had forced close to 150 travelers to turn back. An event that had lessened the train's numbers from 400 to 250. Toni knew Sam and Blake weren't happy with the smaller train now that they were in a territory where Indians were more likely to become hostile rather than simply ornery. They'd come across some, mainly curious; a few thieves had stolen livestock that had wandered outside the circle; but for the most part, their encounters with the natives had resulted in occasional trade and minor annoyances. Until two days ago. Toni had a sinking feeling that that may have just been the beginning of hostility between the Cheyenne and their wagon train.

By the time Kip returned from his morning scouting expedition with Sam, Toni had breakfast ready. "Sam says to tell you we're in for a washing in a little while, so you best cover anything you don't want getting wet."

Toni couldn't help the flutter in her stomach at the thought of a storm. "Did he say if it's going to be bad?"

"Didn't say." Kip helped himself to the plate Toni held out.

"He probably would have if it was supposed to be bad, right?"

Gulping down a large bite, Kip gave a shrug. "I don't know."

Toni expelled a huff. Why was she even asking a twelve-year-old boy for information? All he cared about was scouting with Blake, Sam, or Mr. Kelley, and stuffing himself with whatever she or Fannie set before him.

Stirring coming from behind distracted her from the clouds and she turned to find Fannie, followed by Katie, exiting the wagon. Fannie frowned. "Is it going to storm?"

"Sam said rain's definitely coming, but according to Kip, he didn't think it was going to be bad."

Fannie nodded, but the frown remained firmly in place.

Toni slipped an arm around her shoulders and gave her a squeeze. "Don't worry. Nothing is going to ruin your wedding day. I wouldn't hear of it." She smiled at the bride. "And you know how firm I can be when I need to be."

Toni could tell Fannie was doing her best to force a smile. To prove she wasn't a bit worried. But Toni saw right through the ruse. Fannie took the plate her friend held out. "I don't see how I'll ever be able to force down a bite." Her gaze flickered to the west. Toni followed her gaze. She tensed as a streak of lightning brought a blast of thunder. Katie screamed and slid beneath the wagon.

Toni caught Fannie's trouble gaze just before her friend stooped down in front of the wagon. "Katie, honey. You come on out now. This storm isn't a twister. Sam says it's not even going to be that bad."

Watching the scene in front of her, Toni couldn't help but remember that awful storm that had taken several lives among the travelers. Poor Katie. She and Becca Kane had been playing together when the twister invaded their quiet world of make believe. In a moment all too real, Katie had been forced to watch as the wind caught little Becca up and tossed her broken body yards away, her spirit already floating to heaven before she hit the ground. Katie was far from over the incident, and even the gentlest of sprinkles caused her anxiety. A storm—albeit mild—terrified her.

Kip set aside his empty plate and knelt on the ground,

dropping to his hands and knees beside the wagon. "Aw, Katie. This ain't nothin' but a little summer storm."

Katie's terrified silence screamed into the saturated air. Fannie's voice trembled a little as she spoke. "Katie, don't you want to come out and climb into the wagon until the rain stops? You'll be more comfortable."

Fannie moved as though she was going to crawl under the wagon with her little sister.

Toni touched her shoulder. "Don't get under there. You'll get dirty and there may not be opportunity for a bath before your wedding. I'll go."

Without waiting for consent, Toni lay on her belly and slid under the wagon, joining Katie. "Sweetheart. I'm going to stay right here with you until the storm is over, okay?"

Toni slipped her arms securely around Katie's shaking body. "We'll be okay, Fannie. You and Kip should go inside and wait it out."

Toni could sense the hesitation in her friend. After all, Fannie had been taking care of her sister and brother since their mother had died three years ago and had almost lost them forever when she had been kidnapped along with Toni. She'd been even more protective since then. "Truly, Fannie," Toni said. "It'll be fine. I'm already here."

"Are you sure?" Fannie asked. The thought that Fannie would even allow her to take care of Katie warmed Toni to her core. Toni nodded.

"Come on, Kip," Fannie said.

Kip hung back, clearly distressed at the thought of leaving his twin sister.

Fannie tugged on his arm a little. "Toni's taking care of her." The sky opened up and poured down on the group of travelers. Kip rose with a swift nod.

"I'll be just inside, Katie," he called. "You ought to get inside the wagon."

"It's okay, Kip." Toni waved him away. "Go before you get soaked."

"Should I Katie?"

The terrified child nodded and Kip slowly rose and walked away.

In the wet and mud, Toni held the trembling child until the rain let up, the storm passed over, and only a few puddles reminded the travelers there had ever been a storm in the first place. But no amount of coaxing from Kip or Fannie could convince Katie to crawl out from underneath the wagon, so Toni stayed, muddy, wet, and miserable, and waited out the soul-robbing fear that she knew the little girl was experiencing. She knew what it was like to curl up in a corner while the rain beat down and people walked by not caring about a young girl, violated and left on the street.

She wouldn't let Katie face this alone.

She had been a couple of years older than Katie was now when Micah Lyons breezed onto her father's farm, a drifter looking for work. By the time harvest ended, Toni's heart had been stolen, along with her innocence. Micah's promise of marriage ended abruptly with her news of pregnancy. He left under the cover of darkness and Toni never saw him again. With mounting fear of discovery, Toni took money from her mama's egg jar, boarded a train for St. Louis, and lost the baby a week later. But she was too afraid, too ashamed to return home, and when Amelia had found her on the street, shivering, ill from the miscarriage and half-starved, Toni didn't think twice about accepting her charity. It was only after she recovered, fattened up, and got some color back in her cheeks that she realized there is no such thing as true charity, and so she went to work in Amelia's bordello. Had it truly been seven years ago? It seemed more like an eternity.

"Why are you crying, Miss Toni?"

Katie's words brought her from her reverie and she looked down at the beautiful blue eyes staring at her with concern.

"I didn't know I was," she replied honestly.

"Did the storm scare you too?"

"No. I was just having a bad memory, that's all." Toni smiled, and firmly pushed back any thoughts of her past. Anything before this moment didn't exist. And she was determined not to allow the pain of those memories again.

Toni's legs trembled a little as she stood with the other spectators within the confines of Fort Laramie, and watched as Blake and Fannie exchanged vows before God and the company of observers. Inside the fort's chapel, Fannie looked beautiful in the gown of deep green with just a touch of lace at the collar and around each wrist. She would have liked to have sewn some along the bottom of the gown as well, but there wasn't enough to go around, so she had to make do.

Fannie's hair was pinned loosely so that curls sprung around her heart-shaped face. She looked every bit the beautiful bride. The joy on her face when the preacher pronounced her Blake's wife was undeniable. Toni felt a sense of loss that Fannie would no longer share her wagon, but happiness for her friend was stronger than any selfish regret.

The strains of "Aura Lee" were just coming to an end by the time Sam screwed up the courage to get anywhere near Toni, let alone ask her for the honor of a dance.

He'd been watching her throughout the evening. Even though she was snubbed by more than a few women, she remained polite, quiet as she served slices of white cake and lemonade. Keeping her eye on Katie and Kip—no doubt for Miss Caldwell—Mrs. Tanner, rather, she seemed to have a lot on her mind. For one thing, she kept her fingers pressed to the scars on her face as much as possible. Didn't she know they were barely noticeable? Especially when one looked into beautiful, amber-colored eyes that squinted with every smile. Not that she did much of that these days.

Now, for the first time all evening, she was in front of the table and not behind. He could tell this song in particular meant something to her. The haunting melody lifted into the air at the end of a violin bow and she swayed to the music, unconsciously, if he had to guess. Somehow, there he was, standing in front of her, grinning like what he knew was a crazy fool. "Would you do me the honor, Miss Toni?"

She started and her eyes widened. "Oh, you don't have to."

"It would be my honor."

A slow smile tipped her lips. "Why not?"

"Truly?"

"Sam Two-Feathers, are you changing your mind? Don't tell me you're trifling with me."

"No, ma'am." He grinned and nestled his hand into the curve of her waist, taking her hand in his. His shoulder warmed in an instant at the touch of her palm. He led her around the dance floor in what must surely be a dream.

He closed his eyes and took in the scent of baking and smoked meat that clung to her, thinly disguised with a hint of lemon water. She smelled delicious. And he'd have liked nothing better than to bury his face in her hair and get the full effect. But he knew better.

A man's grunt interrupted their moment. Sam opened his eyes to find Mr. Kane sneering at the two of them, his wife Amanda looking more embarrassed than angry.

"Is there a problem, Kane?" he asked.

Mr. Kane didn't even bother to look at him. That alone made Sam bristle. But the man's next words nearly got him licked.

"If you like Indians so much, why not just go with the chief and leave the rest of us alone?"

Toni gasped and stood still in the middle of the dance floor. Her eyes filled with horror.

"Kane," Sam warned. "Where'd you get the whisky?"

"I don't know what you're talkin' about, half-breed."

"Yes, you do. And trust me, the fact that you're drunk is the only thing saving you from getting the thrashing you deserve after speaking to a lady that way."

"Lady?" he spat. "Where'd you get the idea this whore was a lady?"

Before he could rear back and smash his fist into the drunken idiot's face, Toni had fled. Sam wanted to go after her. But he knew he should take care of the staggering, big-mouthed oaf standing in front of him just begging for a fight.

"Sam, take him back to camp and see that he sleeps it off." Blake's command couldn't have come at a worse time. But Sam knew the wagon master was right. Normally, they wouldn't allow anyone who had been drinking to return to camp until they sobered up, but with most of the women and young children remaining inside the walls of the fort until they pulled out, Kane's wagon seemed to be the best place for him. Besides, everyone knew the poor man had lost his daughter in that twister, and that knowledge somehow made it easier to forgive his transgressions. For now. But Sam wasn't sure how much longer he'd be able to look the other way.

Toni bit her lip to keep from giving in to the tears clogging her throat as she started clearing dishes and left over refreshments from the table. "Why'd you let him get away with talking to you like that?"

She didn't even have to look up from the refreshment table to know the young woman from the night before had followed her. "Because not everything is worth fighting over." Toni peered at the woman.

"Did you hear what he called you?"

Toni gave her a steady look. "Yes."

For the first time, the woman's demeanor cracked as she obviously caught Toni's meaning. Her face glowed and she cleared her throat. "I-um-well—I see. You're a . . ."

"*Was*." Toni raised her chin, surprised at the pride welling inside of her. She truly wasn't that and she wouldn't be called it again. Maybe some things were worth fighting over, after all. "Not anymore."

The young woman seemed relieved. She nodded.

Toni scraped a dish of half-eaten cake into the refuse pile. "What did you say your name is?"

"I didn't, but it's Ginger." She wiped her palm against dirty buckskin trousers and offered her hand.

"Pleased to meet you, Ginger. I'm Toni."

"Want some help cleaning up this mess?"

"Sure. If you wouldn't mind." Toni nearly dissolved into tears at the kindness. Even if it was from a rough young woman with heaven knew what sort of background.

But who was Toni to look down on anyone for any reason? And what was wrong with Ginger dressing in buckskins and wearing a gun belt? Did that make her less a person? Did it make her less a woman? Did it mean she wasn't worthy of a man's love or a kind word?

"Excuse me a minute, Ginger. I have something to take care of. I'll be back."

"If you're going where I think you're going, I'm coming with you. These dishes can just wait until we get back."

"Suit yourself."

With her new friend Ginger on her heels, Toni stomped with purpose toward Sam and Mr. Kane. The wagon scout was practically carrying the drunken fool out the gate.

"Hold on a second, Sam," Toni said firmly.

"Everything okay?" the scout asked.

"No." Toni planted her hands on her hips and stood, feet firm as though bracing for a heavy wind. "Everything is not okay."

"What on earth are you doing, Toni Rodden?" Mr. Kane's wife, Amanda, gave a little stance of her own.

"This doesn't concern you, Amanda."

The woman drew her shawl about her and stuck her nose in the air. "If it concerns my husband and the likes of you, it concerns me."

"I ain't had nothin' to do with her, Mandy. Don't believe her."

"Don't be a fool." Toni sniffed her disdain and looked down on Amanda and then Mr. Kane, himself. "Amanda, you've known me for months now. Better than most of the women have even bothered to try to get to know me. How can you even suggest I might be cozying up to your husband?"

Amanda averted her gaze, but not before Toni noted shame filling her eyes.

"Toni, can this wait until morning?" Sam said quietly, indicating with his head that they had already drawn a crowd.

"No. No it can't, Sam. I plan to have my say." She panned the crowd. "And you all might as well listen."

"You don't have anything to say we want to hear." Someone called from the crowd.

"Shut up and let her talk," Ginger hollered, her hand on her Colt. "Or you'll answer to me."

The crowd grew silent. Ginger nodded at Toni. "Go ahead, say your piece."

"Thank you." Toni's gaze nailed Mr. Kane, whose face slouched in drunken stupidity. "Now, Mr. Kane. All of you! I work as hard on this wagon train as the rest of you. I pick up buffalo chips, haul water, cook, and do just about anything that is asked of me."

"What's that got to do with anything?" a woman's voice called from the crowd. "So do the rest of us."

Ginger cleared her throat loudly and fingered her Colt. The woman took the hint and closed her mouth.

"And that is my point exactly. Each of us has a different past. Mine was harder to hide. And yes, I was not the sort of woman you want your sons marrying. Fine. I don't want them anyway. As far as who I was before, that's all behind me. And any decent Christian man or woman knows that God has forgiven my trespasses. So say what you want behind my back. Call me all the names in your twisted, bitter little hearts. Brush your skirts aside when you see me coming. I don't care. But I will not! I repeat, I will not stand by and listen to any of you calling me 'whore' or inferring that I'm going to resume my former life as soon as we get to Oregon. I have as much right to be treated with dignity as the rest of you. We share an equal load of work and responsibility and I deserve to share in an equal amount of respect. And that's all I intend to say on the matter. But know this, I will not sit by and allow you to degrade me one more day."

So saying, she swung around and faced the man who had begun the entire encounter. "And that means you, too!"

Without another word, she brushed past Ginger and stomped away. Ginger followed, bursting into laughter. "That drunken idiot looked like he didn't know what hit him."

Toni took little pleasure in the victory. If she truly had just won a victory. All she wanted was to be treated like a person with value. Not a whore. She shoved her hands into the sudsy dishwater.

Ginger gave a grunt. "There's ladies comin'." Her voice was thick with disdain. Toni could guess Ginger hadn't been treated much better than she had at the hands of proper "ladies."

Toni looked up and tensed at the sight of five women, including Mrs. Brady, the Captain's wife from the fort and Harriet Lamb, the preacher's wife, coming toward her.

Mrs. Brady gave her a kind smile. "We thought you could use a hand cleaning up."

Relief swept through her. "Thank you. Ginger and I would appreciate it."

Mrs. Lamb's smile included both Toni and Ginger. "Just tell us what to do."

Quickly, Toni doled out tasks and before long several more women joined the group—most from the wagon train.

Ginger stood next to her and dried dishes as the dozen or so women made short work of cleanup. "Well, I'll be derned."

A smile tipped Toni's lips. "I couldn't have said it better myself."

Six

Toni knew the moment she saw Fannie's face that her wedding night had been everything the young woman could have dreamed of. Such knowledge endeared the rough-edged Blake to Toni, no matter how he felt about her. And he certainly didn't hide the fact that he didn't have much use for her.

He also didn't hide the fact that he was crazy about his new bride. The two of them had walked, hand in hand, into camp just moments earlier. Toni stirred the pot of stew she'd warmed over the fire to feed herself and the twins, then straightened up to face Fannie.

Blake kissed his wife on the cheek then looked at Toni. "Seen Sam around?"

"He rode toward the lake a little while ago."

"I'll be back," he said to Fannie.

Toni gave a short laugh as Fannie sighed, watching her new husband strut like a peacock to get his horse, Dusty, from Kip.

"What's so funny?" Fannie asked with a silly grin. "Oh,

never mind. I have a pretty good idea who you're laughing at."

"Did you come for a visit, or to start packing up your things?"

"Oh, Toni. That's the only difficult part about marrying Blake. Having to leave you all alone."

"I'll be fine. And when we get to Oregon, I'll hand the wagon right over to you." She gave a short laugh. "Provided there's anything left of it after we cross the mountains."

"Don't be silly." Fannie waved toward the wagon that she had spent a whole year saving up for in order to escape the cruel man who had held her as an indentured servant much longer than her contract specified. "I want you to have it. You'll have to have a place to live until you get a home built, anyway. Blake says most people live in their wagons or tents for awhile."

Toni's heart gave a lurch. She hadn't even thought about what she'd do once she got to Oregon. How would she get a house built before winter? She'd have to hire it done, so first she had to take in enough sewing or laundry to pay someone. It was all so overwhelming. "Well, let's get you packed up so you can move to your new wagon."

Toni paused. "Do you want me to keep Kip and Katie here for a few nights?"

Fannie's face grew pink. She shook her head. "I want to get them settled in and used to Blake being part of the family."

Again, Toni's heart gave a lurch. Suddenly she was no longer part of this little family. She had grown so close to Fannie and the twins that she'd truly learned to love them as a sister. But the fact was, she wasn't part of the family. Blake was.

Sam had an idea. He hadn't failed to notice Ginger's near-hero worship of Toni since she told the whole wagon train that she would no longer be treated like a soiled dove. Sam himself had been more proud than he ever thought possible. But he'd be lying if he said he wasn't concerned about Toni being all alone. How would she drive the oxen all alone, take care of her own chores, gather her own water, and so many other things that most families split two, three, four, or even more ways? Most single women, like Miss Sadie, hired camp boys to help with chores, but he knew Toni had no means with which to do so. So after prayer and meditation, Sam had devised a plan. A plan that involved Ginger.

He found her inside the fort, stirring up her own brand of trouble. "What do you think you're doing, mister?" she sputtered, pushing back wet hair from her face. Her eyes blazed with anger. The storekeeper dunked her in the horse trough for what appeared to be not the first time.

"You ever going to steal from me again?"

"I didn't steal!"

He dunked her again and left her under until Sam felt he might have to step in. Thankfully, the man wasn't bent on murder. He let her up. She gasped and coughed. "You varmint. You lowdown snake of a slimy rat-faced pig snout!"

Sam fought back a grin as the group of soldiers watching the event set up a howl of laughter. "Stop laughing!" she screamed. She reached for her Colt and lifted it out of the holster. Her hand shook as she pointed the gun at the store-keeper.

"Hey, now. You put that thing away before you hurt some-one," the grizzled man said.

"You should have thought of that before you dern near drowned me, mister."

Stealthily, Sam moved in. He knew he'd only have one chance to stop the foolish, prideful young woman from doing something that would leave her swinging from the end of a rope.

"You made a big mistake with me, mister," she continued her threatening diatribe.

"Listen, young lady. It's all right. You just go on and keep that licorice. I don't need it."

"I told you. I didn't steal no dadblamed licorice. I was going to pay for it."

Even staring down the barrel of a Colt revolver, the store-keeper couldn't hold back a snort of disbelief.

The girl's shaking hand suddenly steadied and Sam made his move. Just as the gun fired, Sam threw off her aim and the bullet plugged a nearby pole. "What the . . ."

The storekeeper's eyes were wide and all traces of amuse-ment had gone.

Ginger whipped around and glared at Sam. "What do you think you're doing? I missed on purpose. I ain't no murderer."

Sam smiled, took hold of her shoulders, and turned her around. He leaned closer to her. "Shut up. Come with me."

"I don't go anywhere with strange men. And I especially don't shut up."

She tried to get loose, but he held her fast, knowing by the outrage growing on the faces of the men in the crowd that the next few seconds would be key in this woman's future. "Do not be foolish."

"Foolish? How foolish is it to sneak up behind a girl with a gun, you crazy half-breed."

"If you insult my mother and father once more, I'll leave you to these men," he whispered against her ear.

She seemed to notice the anger for the first time. Sam heard her gulp. "For mercy's sake. No offense meant."

"She ain't going nowhere." The storekeeper stepped forward.

"Listen folks. Let's be reasonable. Now, this little girl isn't worth getting in an uproar over."

The poor private who had been standing closest to the pole that now held a healthy sized slug, shot forward. "She blamed near killed me."

"H-he threw off my aim. I-I wasn't really going to shoot anyone."

"She's a thief." The storekeeper had lost all sense of grace. "And would have killed me if she could have shot a straight line."

A gasp tore through Ginger's throat and Sam clapped his hand over her mouth before she could blurt out whatever she was thinking.

"Listen, obviously there's been a mistake," Sam said, trying to keep his voice calm. "Miss Ginger didn't mean any harm." He was almost certain, anyway.

"Maybe not. But she caused her share just the same." The storekeeper looked around at the highest-ranking soldier in their midst—a lieutenant who, from what Sam could tell, might have just started shaving a year ago. "What do you plan on doin' about this attempt on my life?"

The soldier looked like he'd rather die than arrest a lady. "Are you sure you want to press charges?"

"You know I do! Else why'd I be askin' what you intend to do about it?"

The lieutenant swallowed hard and stepped forward, his face clouded with dread for the task he was being forced to carry out. Sam stepped in front of Ginger. "Listen, folks. How about if I take this young lady off your hands once and for all?"

"You ain't taking me anywhere half-br—mister." At least she was a fast learner.

"That's right. I want justice." The storekeeper didn't look like he was in any mood to be reasonable short of "justice." But Sam couldn't leave Ginger at the mercy of a mob of irritated men.

"Mr. Lyons," the lieutenant said. "Perhaps we can let the young lady leave with the wagon train with Mr. . . . uh,"

"Two-Feathers." Sam smiled.

"Mr. Two-Feathers." He turned back to the storekeeper, his eyes almost pleading. "I see no reason to detain the lady. There was no real harm done, was there?"

"I promise I'll never set foot in this fort again." Finally, the young woman had realized how dire her situation was about to become. "I-I truly was going to pay for the licorice, but I got sort of distracted by something outside the window and I forgot I had it in my hand."

"It's all right, Ginger," Sam assured her. "All you have to do is pay for it now and I'm sure Mr. Lyons—was it?—will let you go."

"Uh," she cleared her throat and leaned in close. "I don't exactly have any money."

"Then how were you plannin' to pay for the licorice?" the storekeeper demanded.

Ginger sent a scowl around the crowd. "Fine. I wasn't going to actually pay for it." She swung around to Sam. "Happy?"

"I'll pay for the licorice." Sam turned to the sound of Grant Kelley's voice. He reached into his vest pocket. "How much does she owe you, sir?"

"Two bits." The storekeeper took a breath. "And another two bits for the trouble."

Ginger gasped. "That's highway robbery! You belong in jail!"

Sam pressed her elbow and murmured. "Easy, Miss Ginger."

Grant Kelley didn't even blink at the ridiculous price. Rather, he turned over the coins and nodded to Sam and Ginger. "Ready to go?"

"I'm not going anywhere with you two."

"Miss Ginger, I have a proposition for you."

"No thanks. I'm not that sort of woman."

"And I'm not that sort of man."

"Then we understand each other. If you'll excuse me, I'll just be pushing on."

Before Sam could detain her, Grant grabbed her arm in an iron grip. "Would you shut up for once and just listen to the man?"

"Thank you, Grant." Sam turned to the stunned woman. "Ride along with us to the wagon train and at least hear me out. If you're not interested, you're free to go."

She scrutinized him, perusing his expression. Sam highly doubted she'd have known if he had been lying, but he had to admire her for at least thinking it through before agreeing.

"All right, Mr. Two-Feathers, I'll go with you." She glared at Grant. "I'm not going because of you."

Grant's lips twitched. "I won't presume to believe you have anything but the deepest of disdain for me. Although I'm at a loss to know why."

"Good. Because that's exactly what I have." She frowned. "Disdain, that is. For you. And I got my reasons."

"Thank you for your candor."

Eyes narrowed, she peered closer. "You laughing at me?"

"Why no, Miss Ginger, I'd be afraid of your sharpshooting eye."

"Why, you . . ."

"I'll ride on ahead so the two of you can talk." Grant rode away, leaving Ginger sputtering after him.

"I've never met anyone with such bad manners."

Sam suffocated the urge to laugh out loud. He decided to get straight to the point. "I'd like for you to travel with Toni as her companion."

"Excuse me?"

"Miss Rodden."

"I know who Toni is. But I travel alone."

"What's a woman like you doing all alone in a rough place like Fort Laramie?"

"I reckon that's my business."

"I'll grant you that, miss. But we both know you haven't been at the fort long, which leads me to believe you were waiting for the wagon train. Why would a woman do that if not to join up and travel the rest of the way under the protection of a wagon train the size of ours?"

"My, uh, husband passed away not long ago. We live a few miles from here. I only go into the fort to trade."

She was lying again. Sam didn't even have to wonder. It seemed just about every time she opened her mouth a falsehood flew out.

"Supposing you do have a place."

"You calling me a liar?"

Sam sucked in a breath. He reined in his horse and grabbed her bridle. He commanded Ginger's gaze. "I don't want to insult you. But yes, I'm guessing you're not telling the truth. That no husband died recently and you don't have a ranch anywhere near here."

Her face reddened. "I never said it was a ranch."

"Are we ready to be honest with each other?"

"All right, fine. I want to stay close to the train. I wasn't going to ask to travel with you though, because I didn't want to have to do chores. Satisfied?"

"Toni needs a companion. Someone to talk to during the day, and divvy up the chores when we set up camp each night. What do you say?"

"What's in it for me?"

Sam shook his head. "I can't pay much. But I could come up with a little."

Interest sparked in her eyes. "How much?"

"I'll pay you twenty dollars at the end of the trail as long as you do your share and live up to the bargain."

"Ten now. Ten at the end."

Sam smiled at her audacity. "Five now. Fifteen when we reach Oregon."

The girl nodded and stuck out her hand. "Deal."

Relief sifted through Sam. In his absence, he knew this girl would look after Toni.

"One more thing."

"What's that?"

"Don't ever let her know about our arrangement."

Seven

A sting pinched her neck, and Toni let out a yelp.

"What happened?" On the wagon seat beside her, Ginger fought with the oxen, a lot more successfully than Fannie had, to be honest. Though Toni felt disloyal even entertaining the thought.

"Horseflies. I'd forgotten how miserable those dadburn insects can be." Toni hated to complain, but truth be told, Ginger was getting on her nerves something fierce. The girl had a stench about her and didn't see the need to bathe. A fact Toni had every intention of remedying at the next creek they came to. One way or another.

Toni swatted at her neck again, but it was too late to do anything about the would-be assassin that had targeted, bit, and buzzed away like the tiny harassing bully it was. Bad enough to be layered in dust every single day for the last three months, nearly swept away by gusty prairie winds, but the horseflies . . . they were the worst. Next to Ginger's odor, anyway. Still, she had no real reason to complain, considering the alternative. She preferred the wind and caked-on dust—even the horseflies and Ginger's incessant presence—to the life she'd left behind.

Still, what had Sam been thinking, suggesting this girl for her traveling companion? She didn't like to seem ungrateful, but for goodness sakes, she was very close to losing her breakfast. Not to mention the nonstop conversation. At least Fannie knew the value of silence. Ginger seemed as nervous as a bride on her wedding night.

"That Sam, he prays a lot, don't he?"

Toni followed Ginger's gaze and smiled. Sam sat on his horse, facing the horizon, his head bowed. "Yes, he does."

"I never had much use for it, myself. Prayer, that is." She stopped struggling with the oxen a second, long enough to yank a long piece of straw from her teeth and toss it to the ground. "Near as I can tell, the Almighty never did nothin' for me and my family."

"How can you tell?"

Ginger's eyes narrowed at the question and she stared past the beasts she drove. "I figure if He did, He did a pretty poor job of it. And if that's the case, who needs a God like that tellin' me what to do?"

Something tripped in Toni's heart and she placed a hand on the girl's filthy buckskin shirt. "I can't pretend to know everything about God. Or even much for that matter. But I do know that a few months ago I was a worthless whore in a worthless town with no hope. And now I'm free and looking forward to a future without being forced to do things I don't want to do."

Ginger gave a pointed look toward Toni's scars. "What happened to you?"

The blunt question was like a slap in the face. "Let's just say I have outward scars now instead of heart scars."

"Heart scars?"

"I can't imagine anyone living the way I have without enduring wounds on the inside. I was beautiful on the outside and bleeding on the inside. Now I'm scarred on the outside, but God sees me as beautiful on the inside."

"Who said you ain't beautiful on the outside? Did that half-breed tell you something like that? Or that wagon master. Don't pay no attention to him. He only has eyes for that little red-head."

Toni wasn't used to being championed. And to be championed by this rough girl was disconcerting to say the least. The hot-headed, gun-toting young woman would as quickly plug someone as look at them and Toni certainly didn't want to be responsible for bloodshed. Thankfully, Blake had taken her gun from her. Still . . . the girl had confided that he'd missed an enormous knife she had tucked beneath her shirt—one reason she wouldn't unbutton the jacket and give her body a little air over the cotton shirt beneath.

"Sam has been nothing but a gentleman. As a matter of fact, if he hadn't come after me when the man I ran away from kidnapped me, I'd be dead right now. He helped tend to me and nursed me until I was better."

"Oh." Ginger fell silent. And remained so. The silence was a mercy as far as Toni was concerned, but she had a feeling the girl had gone to a place deep in her memory where her own scars were bleeding.

"Tell me about your family."

Ginger's eyes blazed as she whipped around to face Toni, and for an instant, Toni shrank back.

"I ain't got no family left and there ain't no sense discussing it. So let's just leave it there."

"I understand not wanting to talk. But if you ever change your mind, I'm a good listener. And I don't gossip so your secrets are safe with me."

The girl's doe-like eyes softened for just a minute, then hardened again. "The only safe secrets are the ones no one knows. And I plan to keep all mine right here." She tapped her temple. "So don't try to get me talkin'."

Toni nodded. She truly understood. "I'll just get down and walk for awhile, if you don't mind. When I come back we can trade places."

"You're going to drive these animals?" Toni wasn't crazy about the skepticism in the girl's tone.

"You'd be surprised at the things I'm capable of doing." Toni sent her a wink and a grin and climbed down.

Sam noticed Toni climb down from the wagon, and alarm seized him. They were being followed. Most likely by the Cheyenne war chief Swooping Eagle. The Indian agent, Fitzpatrick, had his own thoughts concerning the settlement of the West. So he wasn't exactly friendly. The agent had confirmed Swooping Eagle had gathered more warriors and would be making one more raid on the wagon train.

Even armed with that, Sam couldn't be sure it was Swooping Eagle. Most of the tribes in these parts were getting restless, even frustrated, with the settlers and even more recently those who were flooding the Black Hills, panning for gold. One thing Sam knew for certain. The wagon train would be meeting up with the band of warriors again before much longer. But the memory of the look on the Cheyenne chief's face when he was forced to ride away without his prize was branded into Sam's memory. And it worried him more than he'd like to admit, despite the time he spent in prayer, searching for wisdom and peace.

Swooping Eagle would not give Toni up without a fight. His pride had been wounded. First by Blake's refusal to trade and second by Toni's own rejection.

Sam knew Toni wouldn't be in any real danger even if Swooping Eagle was successful in his kidnapping attempt. Cheyenne men generally treated their women fairly well. Much like the Sioux, although, as with any race, there were good and bad men among them. But even captives were treated well as long as they did what they were told and didn't cause trouble. Toni's unusual, white-blonde hair would make her something of a curiosity in the tribe. The most that might happen would be someone trying to cut off a lock of her hair. But even that Sam doubted. To be sure, she wouldn't be harmed. But that wasn't the point. Sam wouldn't allow anyone to take Toni against her will.

She'd been through enough heartache. For the rest of her life, as long as he had anything to say about it, she would have a choice.

He debated whether or not he should advise her to stay in the wagon, but ultimately decided against it. No sense in alarming her before he needed to.

Blake rode up next to him. "You saw?"

Sam gave a grim nod.

"How long before they attack?"

"Any time, if they're going to."

No sooner had the words left him than a line of dust rose from the horizon and the faint sound of war cries could be heard. Blake sprang into action. "Circle the wagons!"

Sam spurred his horse and galloped toward Toni. He jerked on the reins and swooped down from the horse. The terror in her eyes shook him to his core. "Come with me," he ordered.

She nodded and took his hand.

"Ginger, get that wagon in place."

"What about my guns?"

"Talk to Blake about that." He had other things to attend to. He led Toni to Sadie Barnes' wagon. "Miss Sadie, we need something to cover her hair. And the two of you duck under this wagon. You have a gun?"

"You know I do." The widow disappeared inside her wagon and returned with a shawl. "Here! Take this."

"Do you think he saw me?" The look of terror in the normally calm, brave woman's eyes pierced Sam's heart. But there was no time to do what came naturally and take her in his arms for comfort. There were more important things at hand. He shook his head in answer to her trembling question.

"I doubt it."

Unless Sam missed his guess, the plan was to kill as many men and make off with as many women as possible. Women and children. With Toni at the top of the list. The Cheyenne camp must not be too far from here. The number of warriors from the other day had grown from twenty to at least two hundred.

This wasn't going to be an easy fight.

Lord, help us, for your glory.

Miss Sadie pointed her finger to Sam's chest. "Get out of here, and go where you'll be most useful. We'll be fine."

Toni stared after Sam, suddenly feeling naked for the first time in months. How could he just ride away like that when he knew the Cheyenne were after her?

"Toni!" Miss Sadie shook her arm. "You have to wake up. Get this on and get under the wagon." Toni nodded and with trembling hands covered her unique hair. "Th-they're getting closer," she whispered.

In moments, the air rang as volley after volley of gunfire blasted the atmosphere and arrows zinged into the air. Toni covered her head and stayed on her belly under Miss Sadie's wagon. She didn't dare look up, afraid that if she did, she'd see the leering, lust-filled eyes of the Indian who wanted her. On the ground next to her, Sadie reloaded her shot gun and fired off another shot, hit her target with a howl and fired off another. Which missed.

She muttered an oath while she reloaded. Then a hasty prayer of repentance. "Honey, get your face out of your hands and help me. Now I got two shot guns, you keep one loaded at all times. This is not time for you to be playing the coward."

Shame tore at Toni's heart. What was she? Some sort of child without the ability to fight back? "You're right, Miss Sadie."

The woman nodded her approval. "Do you know how to load it?"

"I think so."

If memory served, this shot gun resembled the one her father had used to bring down their supper on more occasions than Toni could count. She grabbed the newly emptied gun and went about loading shells into the double chambers. Miss Sadie took it and smiled. "Good girl. Keep 'em comin'."

By some miracle, Toni was able to tune out the chaos around her and focus on the task at hand. After what seemed like hours, but most likely amounted to no more than fifteen minutes, the Indians retreated. Toni nearly wept in relief. "Is it over?"

Miss Sadie looked up from the horizon and focused her gaze squarely on Toni's eyes. "This round."

Toni's stomach dropped. "This round?"

A nod jerked the middle-aged widow's pinned up hair. "They'll carry off their dead, regroup, refocus, and come back strong."

"Wh-when?"

"Probably no more than an hour from now. Maybe sooner."

Toni's ears perked up at the sound of rustling about, the travelers coming out from under wagons and standing up from their hiding places behind wagon wheels. An angry bellow shot through the air and she knew instantly that Ginger was not happy.

"Get this dadburn thing out of my leg."

Toni slithered on her belly toward the nearest opening. But Sadie yanked her back. "No you don't, missy."

"What do you think you're doing? I'm going to help Ginger."

"Nope. You stay here. I'll go check on her."

Toni opened her mouth to argue, but Miss Sadie's glare silenced her. "Now, I know it weren't your fault, Toni," the woman said, expelling a breath. "But that Indian wants you for his squaw and that's what this is all about. It'll be best for everyone if you stay out of sight with your hair covered up until all this nonsense is over and hopefully we can get through the day with as few dead folks as possible."

Eight

Pain, white and hot, sliced through Ginger's thigh. The wagon train folks buzzed past her, none of them appearing to see or hear her, even though she lay out in open view and hollered as loud as she could. Her head was beginning to swim with that sickening feeling just before blackness invaded and unconsciousness became imminent. Her flaw. She fainted at the sight of blood, broken bones, or vomit. And it didn't take much in the way of pain to cause her to swoon. Horror filled her at the thought of anyone discovering this weakness right out in the open while they rushed around and over her in their panic to tend to their own and prepare for the next wave of attack.

Closing her eyes, she fought the tendency to faint, swallowing hard and trying to focus her thoughts around butterflies and flowers. "Miss Ginger?"

Dread shot through her gut as she opened her eyes and raised them from boots to trousers to a buckskin shirt. Grant Kelley.

He stooped down without asking permission. He whipped a knife from his pocket and reached for her buckskin trousers. "What do you think you're doing?" Ginger asked, wishing her voice didn't tremble so.

"Shh. Calm down. You're losing a lot of blood."

"Th-that's not what I asked, mister."

He met her gaze, his soft brown eyes so earnest, it was almost impossible for Ginger to be angry with him in this moment when he seemed to be the only person alive who cared if she lived or died.

"Miss Ginger. Let's get something straight. I'm going to cut away the leg of these trousers, so I can get to the arrow lodged in your thigh."

"Like heck you are!"

A scowl marred his unnervingly handsome face. "Like heck I'm not. Now don't fight me. I'm not going to watch you bleed to death. And this thing is jammed in tight."

Ginger knew when she'd been bested and right now, she didn't have the strength to fight him.

"All right. Do what you have to do. But . . ."

"But what?"

She had planned to say, "but don't tell anyone if I pass out." But no sense borrowing trouble. Maybe the swimming in her head would stop soon.

"Hang on, this is going to hurt."

She stifled a scream just as she drifted into blessed darkness.

* * *

"Here they come again!"

Less than an hour after the first wave of attack ended, the wagon train had regrouped, and patched up their wounded. Thankfully no one had been killed so far, but Sam wasn't sure that was going to last. It depended upon how serious Swooping Eagle was about capturing Toni. If it was even about her anymore.

The war cries filled the horizon as the dust kicked up beneath the thundering of horses' hooves nearly hid the Indians from view until they grew closer. Sam cast one quick glance at Toni, still under the wagon, to assure himself she was safe for the moment. And for the duration, if he had anything to say about it. Arrows filled the air, followed by gunfire. Somehow, half the Indians were carrying rifles. Irritation filled him. How did the government expect to keep the settlers relatively safe if they didn't crack down on the traders illegally selling firearms to the various tribes? Rifles and whisky. These two things could very well mark the demise of the plains Indians. Sam aimed his own rifle and fired at a brave, whose brief, shocked gaze met his just before he slid off his horse, dead as he hit the ground. Grief filled Sam. Another man lost his life without having heard the gospel of Jesus.

Sam scanned the warriors, searching for Swooping Eagle. He would be the one wearing the most ornate war bonnet. Sam knew the only way to stop this onslaught was to wound the leader or kill him outright. Sam preferred the former. As much as he disliked this man who was obsessed with stealing away Toni, he also knew God loved him and wanted to see him embrace salvation rather than lose his life, godless, on the battlefield. Wounding him would stop the battle, but give Swooping Eagle the opportunity to hear the gospel another day.

This onslaught seemed more desperate than the first one. The braves weren't as careful. And the loss of life seemed greater from the first arrow launched toward the wagon train. The settlers had the advantage in that they could take cover behind and under wagons, while their attackers were in the open and more than likely knew the chances of survival were slim.

Sam fired off three more shots, hitting his mark each time, before his eyes came to rest on Swooping Eagle. The warrior noticed him at the same time and charged. Lifting his rifle, Sam aimed as well as he could with the chief bearing down on him. They fired simultaneously. Hot pain knifed through Sam's side just before the ground rose up to meet him.

Toni saw Sam drop and scrambled out from under the wagon before Miss Sadie could stop her. Fannie reached Sam at the same time. "Toni, get back under the wagon. I'll take care of Sam."

"No. You go back to Katie."

"I'm not leaving you!"

"Well, I'm not leaving him."

As the chaos swelled around them, the two women stopped arguing with unspoken agreement and dropped to the ground on either side of Sam Two-Feathers.

"It's a clean wound," Fannie announced. "The bullet went right through. That's good news. But we'll need something to stop the bleeding."

Toni didn't think. She snatched the shawl from her head. "Toni!"

"Don't." Toni was in no mood to be reminded that her hair had gotten the whole lot of them in this mess. She didn't need to be reminded that Sam lay on the ground, possibly dying because of her. She pressed the shawl to the wound.

Thankfully, Fannie let it go. "All right, then. Keep pressure on his wound while I go get needle and thread."

Toni looked down, her heart softening at the blood-drained face of the man who had come to her rescue for the second time. "Live, Sam," she whispered. Pain shot through her scalp and in less than an instant, she was on her feet, dragged by her hair. A scream tore from her throat. "No!" Horrified, she barely had time to register the startling reality of what was happening. The war chief, his arm pouring blood from a bullet wound, stumbled as he attempted to capture her. Toni reacted quickly, knowing her only chance was to strike where he was most vulnerable. She swung with all of her might and landed her hardest punch on the blood-slicked wound. A roar of pain rose from the Indian and he turned her loose. When he whipped around, he was unsteady from pain and blood loss and Toni knew survival meant one thing: she kicked at his leg and at the same time shoved as hard as she could. The tactic worked as he stumbled and landed hard on the ground. Before she could think, another

Indian screamed and raced in their direction. She knew this was the last moment she would be alive. She stood strong, closed her eyes and waited for the end to come.

Only it didn't. She waited but instead of the blow she expected, there was nothing. She opened her eyes and saw the Indian war chief's dark eyes boring into her as his brave hurried him outside of the circle of wagons and hoisted him onto his horse. With a swift command, the chief rounded up the war party, and in moments the battlefield was silent.

Blake walked the circle speaking with the families who had lost loved ones. Six in all. Four men, two women. Among them was Mrs. Cordellia Harrison, wife of Charles and mother to Alfred, a simpleton, and Belinda, a feisty young girl about Kip and Katie's age.

He stopped to pay his respects. "Please accept my condolences, Mr. Harrison," he said to the grieving man. "We'll be holding a joint funeral in the morning, as soon as everyone has time to prepare the bodies."

Belinda's tear-streaked face peeked up from where she stood over her mother's body.

"I'd like to bury Mother in her wedding gown, would that be okay Mr. Tanner?"

Touched by her grief, he patted the girl's head. "I think that would be real nice, Lindy. You go right ahead and do that. Provided your pa has no objections."

"I don't care one way or another," he said. "The girl can do as she pleases."

Alfred, sixteen years old, sat on the wagon tongue, watching his mother as though trying to wrap his mind around what had happened. Blake went to him and slung an arm around the lad's shoulders. "You doing okay, Alfred?"

"Ma's dead," he said bluntly. "I guess she ain't cookin' supper."

"I guess not, son," Blake said. "You come to my wagon and Miss Fannie will cook you a good meal."

"If it's okay with Pa." Alfred looked at his dad, the innocence in his clear blue eyes moving Blake. Mr. Harrison wasn't always the most patient of men. Blake had heard him yelling his frustrations at the lad on more than one occasion. Alfred might have the body of a boy, nearly grown, but his mind would never grow beyond the child he was. It was obvious to anyone that the boy's pa didn't have much use for him. And the deceased mother had adored the simple, sweet lad.

Blake turned to Mr. Harrison, whose gaze rested on Alfred.

"Mr. Harrison? How about the three of you join my wife and me for dinner?"

"Huh?" the man looked up, as though startled. Then he nodded. "Oh, sure, sure. Thank ya kindly. We'll be there."

Blake continued his surveillance of the wagon train. There were more wounded than he'd expected. But his heart nearly stopped when he found Sam on the ground. Toni next to him, her hands slick with blood as she sewed up a gash in his side.

"What happened?" He felt foolish as soon as the words left his mouth. Of course his friend had been wounded in battle.

"The chief shot him," Fannie said. "But the bullet went straight through, so we just have to hope for the best. He's been in and out of consciousness a couple of times in the last few minutes."

Blake nodded, satisfied his friend was receiving the best possible care. He focused on Toni. "Keep me updated on his condition."

"I will."

He turned to Fannie. "We're having the Harrison's for dinner. Is that a problem?"

As soon as he saw the incredulous look in her eyes, he knew he was in trouble.

"Blake! After everything we've been through, you're inviting folks to supper? You know how horrible I cook!"

"I don't think they'll care, sweetheart."

"What do you mean?"

"Mrs. Harrison was killed in the attack."

In a beat, compassion swept away the irritation on her freckled face. "Oh, Blake. I'm so sorry." She nodded. "I'll throw something together even if I have to ask Miss Sadie to supper just so she'll do the cooking."

Blake bent and kissed his wife. She melted against him, only for a second, allowing him to give her strength. Blake's heart nearly beat out of his chest at the simple gesture of trust. He loved this woman with every fiber of his being and marveled that she loved him too. She pulled away. Smiled. Pressed the palm of her hand to his chest. "I'll be fine. You should go check on the rest of the train."

Reaching forward, Blake cupped her cheek in his palm. "I love you, Mrs. Tanner."

She blushed and gave a shy smile. "I love you too, Mr. Tanner. Now, go and make yourself useful."

"Yes, ma'am."

Blake walked away, chuckling to himself. God surely had given him better than he deserved.

Nine

Sam awoke to someone moaning close by. It only took a minute for him to realize the sound came from his own throat. Then it all came back to him. Swooping Eagle had shot him at the same time his gun had fired. Had he killed the warrior? Or had the Cheyenne. . .

"Toni?"

"I'm here, Sam."

Relief flooded through him. "Thank God you're safe."

She loomed above him, wiping his brow with a soothing, cool cloth. "I'm not the one you need to be concerned about right now."

"Swooping Eagle?"

"He's still alive," she said grimly. "At least he was when they carried him off. You shot him in the arm, but it was bleeding a lot."

"Where am I?"

"My wagon. You've been here for three days."

Alarm shot through him and he tried to sit up. Pain seared

his side causing him to suck in a sharp breath. "I can't stay here, Miss Toni."

"Don't be silly. You can't get up. It took three men to get you settled into the wagon in the first place. If you try to move, you'll open that wound and we'll have to start all over again."

"It is not right for me to stay." How could she be so careless? "You've worked too hard to redeem yourself, Miss Toni. This doesn't look right."

"Sam," she said slowly, smiling down at him. "Do you honestly think I have a reputation to protect? No one in this wagon train will think any better of me if I throw you out of the wagon and leave you to care for yourself. Which, by the way, you are in no shape to do anyway. Blake approves of the arrangement so there's really nothing you can say about it." Her lips curved into a soft smile as she softened the blow. "Ginger and I are sleeping in a tent just outside. So don't worry. I'm not going to be sleeping in here while you are."

He smiled. "Good."

"Are you in pain?"

"Yes."

"All we have to help is whiskey. I could bring you some if you want."

Again he smiled. "Indians and whiskey don't mix well. And even if I didn't have Indian blood, I have convictions against drinking liquor."

Her face darkened to red. "I'm sorry. I shouldn't have offered."

On impulse, Sam took her hand. "You were being thought-ful."

She snatched her fingers away as though his touch caused her pain. "I'll be back in a few minutes with some soup. Try to rest in the meantime. It-it'll help with the pain if you stay unconscious until you're better."

Sam closed his eyes, berating himself for not thinking before he intertwined his fingers with hers. She must think he was taking advantage of their precarious situation. He would force himself to stay awake so that when she returned he could apologize.

Toni's hands trembled and her stomach fluttered as she climbed down from the wagon. Being this close to a man in such an intimate setting had bothered her more than she had anticipated. But she had to be strong for now. Remind herself that Sam wouldn't take advantage of her. Even if he had the strength to do so.

"Toni!" From inside their tent, Ginger bellowed for the tenth time in less than an hour.

With a weary sigh, Toni slipped into the tent. "What is it this time, Ginger?"

"Well, for mercy's sake, you don't have to be hateful about it do ya? I ain't exactly here cause I want to be, ya know."

"I'm sorry, Ginger. You're right. What can I do for you?"

"I can't get this dadburned pillow to sit right at my neck. I feel like I'm getting a crick or something."

"Here, let me help." Toni remained calm as she adjusted the feather pillow. "Better?"

A smile broke out on the young woman's face and Toni couldn't help but notice what a pretty girl she could be. One thing was for certain, she would have to be bathed now. And with Toni playing caretaker, the girl had no choice but to accept the inevitable.

"I'm getting some buffalo stew for Sam. I'll bring you some first if you can eat on your own."

"Why couldn't I? It's my leg ailin', not my arms."

"All right then, I'll be back in a few minutes." Toni stopped and then turned as though she'd just had a thought. "I've managed to round you up a fresh set of clothing."

"I ain't wearin' a dress." She faced Toni with one eyebrow raised and folded her arms across her chest for emphasis. "Never have. Never will."

Toni had to wonder about a girl that had never worn a dress. At least Fannie had only taken to wearing trousers as a way to manage the harsh trail. And she had recently discovered bloomers worked just as well and most of the women on the trail wore them, so Blake didn't object.

Toni focused her attention back to Ginger. "It's all right. I wouldn't dream of asking you to wear a dress. As a matter of fact, Fannie's given up trousers and has a couple of pair for you."

A smile broke out across her face. "That's fine. Tell her thank-e-kindly. Once this dadburn leg heals up enough, I'll wear them proudly."

"Oh, one more thing. I'm not giving you the trousers unless you take a bath."

Ginger's jaw dropped. "Wha . . . ? Are you daft? I can't be

gettin' my leg in no water. The shock'd likely kill me."

"Relax. I wouldn't dream of getting you in the water just yet."

"Don't scare me like that then."

"When you're ready for clothes. THEN you'll have a bath."

Ginger scowled. "You're bossy."

"You have no idea." Toni gave a chuckle. "I'll bring your supper right away."

"No hurry. I lost my appetite just thinking about a bath. Feed Two-Feathers first."

Blake waited two more days before visiting Sam. He figured after almost a week, his friend was up to a visitor and he needed some answers. He slipped inside the wagon and watched as Sam's chest rose and fell in a steady rhythm that indicated he slept peacefully.

Instinct, born of years as a tracker, trained to be alert even in sleep, opened Sam's eyes. He blinked at Blake. "I was beginning to think you'd forgotten about me."

Blake grinned. "Under strict orders from your nurse. Toni refused to allow me to set foot in here until you were strong enough."

"Then I suppose it's good news for me that you're here."

"I'm allowed ten minutes and three are gone."

"The Cheyenne?"

"Haven't seen hide nor hair of them since the attack."

"Miss Toni said I shot Swooping Eagle in the arm. He's probably already planning another attack."

Blake shrugged. He'd been worried about the same thing. Especially since they'd been sitting, exposed, at the foot of the Black Hills since the battle. "How long before you're up to sitting a horse?"

"Now."

"Let's give it a little more time."

Sam gave a heavy sigh. "We've lost more time on this trail than any since we've been doing this together. We left out of Independence nearly four months ago. The longest it's ever taken to get a train to the valley is five months. But from the looks of it it's going to be at least another three."

Blake didn't deny it. "We'll be all right, as long as we make it through the South Pass in the next couple of weeks. Any later and we'll be forced to backtrack and camp outside of Fort Laramie until spring."

"I don't want to take any chances with Toni." Sam's firm tone confirmed what Blake had suspected for some time.

"You planning to ask her to marry you?"

A frown marred Sam's brow and for a moment, Blake wondered if he was wrong.

"Miss Toni is a white woman. She isn't for the likes of me."

Blake gave a short laugh. "Do you honestly think she's too good for you? The woman was a . . ."

"Don't say it." Sam's eyes glittered with warning. "Toni is a good woman. She deserves a chance at a new life."

Blake knew there was no point in arguing. He figured Toni had probably changed, right enough, but the proof would be after they arrived in Oregon and the real work began. Then they'd see if she was going to return to her former profession. But no point in bringing that up again and making Sam all defensive when the tracker needed all of his energy to get well. "Even if she has changed for good, the fact remains that she isn't any better than you are, Sam. You've lived your life as a good, Christian man. A white man. And you have a right to marry the woman you love if she loves you too, and she'd be a downright fool not to."

Sam gave him a weak smile. "I only have a right to marry the woman God says I have a right to marry."

"And that can't be Toni?"

"I don't see how."

"Well, that's up to you to decide." Blake wasn't someone to be involved in the dealings of the heart. All he cared about for now was getting his friend well enough to travel.

Toni heard enough of Sam's conversation with Blake to realize he didn't see a match between them ever working. It was just as well that Sam felt that way, but hearing the words from his lips cut deeply just the same. She had known for months that Sam would never see her as a suitable match, but to hear him flatly say to Blake that God wouldn't approve of a relationship between the two of them more than proved to Toni that it was time for her to stop wondering if perhaps . . . just maybe . . . there might ever be something special between them. The memory of his arms plagued her. She'd hoped that eventually he might be able to love her. Now she knew once and for all that would never ever happen. Her role in Sam's life right now was nothing more than a nurse. She raised her chin and wiped her eyes and made a decision . . . never again would she think about a man as a suitor.

Suitor. What a jest. The only suitor she had ever had was Micah. And all he'd done was steal her innocence and send her into a life of prostitution.

Sam was right. He was too good for her.

"Toni!"

With a sigh, Toni went to the tent where Ginger still lay unable to move around too much. Toni stopped short as she entered. Grant Kelley stood next to her, his lips pursed into a scowl that bespoke his frustration.

"Good evening, Mr. Kelley," Toni said. "Is there anything I can do for you?"

"He's trying to get me to use that thing," Ginger huffed, pointing to a funny-looking crutch, rough-hewn from branches. "He wants to kill me."

"Thunderation, woman," Grant exploded. "All I wanted to do was help. But don't use the dadblamed thing. If you prefer to be an invalid."

He let the crutch fall to the ground with a thud and a puff of dust. He whipped around, slid past Toni and exited the tent without another word.

"Ignorant man," Ginger muttered. "I'll be hanged if I ever take anything from that man."

Toni shrugged. She walked across the tent and picked up the crutch. "It was a kind thing to do. This might actually help you get up and around soon."

"I'll die before I use it."

"That's awfully stubborn of you considering he was just

trying to be kind. Besides, you've been complaining about cabin fever. Here's your chance to get out of here. Why be so bullheaded?"

"Bullheaded, my eye. Smart is what I'm being. That man doesn't do anything without a reason. Believe me. I know."

Toni smiled. Was it possible Ginger had taken a fancy to the dashing former sheriff?

She was about to ask, when Fannie appeared. "Hi, you two."

"Hi," Ginger muttered.

Fannie lifted an eyebrow. "What's the matter?"

Ginger scowled, turning her head without answering.

"Mr. Kelley fashioned a crutch for Ginger to use so she can get around."

"Sounds like he's sweet on you, Ginger."

The scowl deepened. "Take it back," she said through clenched teeth.

"Why should I?" Fannie laughed. "And besides, why should it upset you? He's handsome, hardworking, kind. Everything a woman could ask for in a husband."

"Husband!"

Toni thought Ginger would explode. The girl swung her legs around to the side of the cot, groped for the crutch, and used it to stand. She hopped on one leg until she stood directly in front of Fannie. "There's a lot you don't know about Grant Kelley. If I had my way, he'd be strung up on the closest tree. So don't try to tease me as though he means something to me. I despise him. And I won't be happy until he's dead."

So saying, the girl maneuvered the crutch and exited the tent for the first time in a week.

In bewildered silence, Toni and Fannie watched her leave. "What do you think that was all about?"

Toni gave a shrug. "I have no idea. I've stopped trying to figure out that girl." She took in the welcome sight of her friend. "What brings you to my part of camp? I've hardly seen you at all since the attack."

"Blake has me cooking for all the families who lost loved ones."

"But you don't cook."

Fannie sighed. "I know. So far Miss Sadie has been doing most of the cooking. But she's under the weather tonight. So I'm in need of some help." She gave Toni a hopeful look. "I hate to put something else on your shoulders. But I truly don't know how I'll feed twenty people without help."

Toni owed this young woman everything. If Fannie hadn't agreed to let Toni come along when she left Hawkins with her brother and sister, Toni would still be working in the rooms above George's saloon. Fixing a meal for twenty folks or so was a small price to pay for Fannie's generosity and friendship.

"What should I fix?"

Relief crossed Fannie's face. "Some of the men went hunting this morning. We have venison to roast. And Blake traded a few pelts for some potatoes when we were at Fort Laramie. Is that all right?"

At the very mention of a venison roast and real potatoes Toni's mouth began to water. "I'll walk with you now. We should get it started if we're going to have supper at a decent hour. It'll take awhile for the venison roast to tenderize."

The two women exited the tent and turned their steps toward Fannie's wagon. "I sure wish I knew why Ginger insists she can't abide Mr. Kelley," Toni said. "Do you think they knew each other before Ginger showed up at Fort Laramie?"

Fannie gave a shrug. "I didn't like Blake in the beginning and he didn't much care for me either. But I had never laid eyes on him until he walked into Tom's store that day. So maybe they just don't cotton to each other."

"I wonder . . ." Toni scanned the circle of wagons until her eyes came to rest on Grant Kelley. She shook her head. The man didn't even notice the stir he caused as he walked by a group of gossiping young belles. "He's awfully handsome, isn't he?"

"Who? Sam?"

"I meant Mr. Kelley."

Fannie snapped to and followed Toni's gaze. "I suppose so. But what about Sam?"

"What do you mean, Fannie?"

The young bride gave a frustrated huff. "I don't think you should be looking at Grant Kelley. Sam's a good man."

Resentment welled inside of Toni. "I'm not looking at any man *that* way. I was just observing how Mr. Kelley doesn't seem to even notice how he's causing a flutter among those young women. And as far as Sam is concerned . . . you're right. He is good. Too good for me and he knows it. So let's just leave him out of these types of conversations from here on out. Shall we?"

Toni's lungs burned and she realized as she gasped for air that she'd spoken so fast, rushing her words, that she hadn't taken time to breathe.

Fannie's lips twisted into a knowing grin.

"I mean it, Fannie." Toni stopped and faced her friend. "I have resigned myself to living alone and I don't want or need to get ideas of romance in my head."

As a woman, she had at her disposal ways to get a man interested. And as a woman of her former profession, she knew even more tricks than the average female, but those things weren't an option. She cared too much for Sam to manipulate him into loving her.

Ten

After a seven-day delay, the wagon train was finally ready to move forward again. Calluses had to re-form, muscles that had grown soft had to once again be hardened. Toni kept a watchful eye on Sam as he slowly, day-by-day acclimated to the saddle so that he'd be ready to ride by the time the wagon train moved out.

Although Toni thought he should rest this evening before they pulled out in the morning, he had insisted upon sharing from the Bible, something he'd been too weak to do thus far. He stood before the group of pioneers, visibly weak and pale. Bible in hand, he flipped through the well-worn pages until he reached the page he was looking for. Peace settled over his features as be began to read. "The Spirit of the Lord God is upon me . . ."

Toni listened in rapturous silence. The poetic words fed into her soul, and she could even imagine the voice speaking was God himself. She became lost in the image of Jesus, anointed by God to heal the brokenhearted, to give beauty into a life where filth and sin had once marred even the most lovely of hearts. The way hers had been before Micah showed up. So pure, so innocent. Innocence quickly gave way to experience and that's where the filth and sin entered. Would she ever feel clean again?

What had become of Mama and Papa? Did they ever think of her? And if so, were their thoughts good or evil? Did they hate her? Did her brother, Jacob? He was almost a man now. Had her sister Emma given birth to a second or third child? She had been heavy with her first baby when Toni left home. Did Emma ever mention their Aunt Toni?

She emitted a sigh. Lately, her thoughts often led her home to the Missouri farm where she was raised. How she longed to return to that time before she had been so foolish as to believe a man.

". . . to set at liberty them that are bruised."

Tears shot to her eyes as the very bruises she should be free from began to ache so much that heaviness descended and she had difficulty taking a breath.

A hand on her arm brought her back to the present and she turned to find Ginger staring, a deep frown marring her brow. "What the heck's wrong with you?"

Toni flashed a glance about the makeshift congregation. Sure enough, Ginger's voice had carried and had even caught Sam's attention. He frowned, but his wasn't like the rest. It wasn't condemning or critical or downright angry. His was one of concern. Was she all right? What was wrong?

His concern felt good. She had to admit. She sent him the

slightest of smiles just to reassure him and he went back to his message.

"Jesus came to give us not only salvation and the assurance of heaven, but also to heal our wounds, physical or emotional, and especially spiritual."

Ginger gave a snort. "He ain't seen fit to do no healin' on this leg of mine," she muttered. She adjusted her body against the tree she sat in front of. For emphasis, she folded her arms across her chest.

"Hush, Ginger," Toni hissed.

The young woman scowled. "So-rry. Maybe I should just leave."

Toni leaned over. "You shouldn't leave. You should stop making a spectacle of yourself and extend Sam the courtesy of shutting your mouth."

Toni half expected the stubborn girl to struggle to her feet and haul herself back to the wagon. Instead, she shut her mouth, tightly, and glared ahead, refusing to so much as look in Sam's direction, or Toni's for that matter, but at least she stayed. And as far as Toni was concerned that showed real progress.

The trail was even slower after Fort Laramie. The positive part of the experience was the ability to travel next to the river. But the weary band knew that as soon as they reached the Red Buttes, another water crossing was imminent. No more happy about the crossing than the rest of the travelers, Fannie's thoughts returned to her near-drowning more than a month earlier. On the wagon next to her, Katie sat, tense, her face drained of all color.

"Don't worry, sweetie," she tried to assure her sister. "Blake says we're building rafts this time. We won't have to swim the oxen across. And just look." She pointed at the beautiful red buttes directly across the river, the red rock even more pronounced by the sun beating down as it signaled its slow departure. "Soon we start heading over the mountains and after that we'll be in Oregon. But first we have to cross the river." And travel another 1,000 miles. But there was no sense in bringing that up for now

"Are we getting ready to cross now?" Katie's voice shook with dread.

"No. We're going to make camp a little early and the men will get to work building some rafts. Then tomorrow we'll start making our way across. And then we'll either move right ahead the following day, or we'll stop to fortify the wagons and make sure they're strong enough to make it the rest of the way to Oregon."

Katie swallowed hard and attempted a nod but she didn't look convinced.

Fannie gave her a playful nudge. "Smile, sweetie. Has God let anything bad happen to us since we escaped from Tom?"

She cleared her throat. "You almost drowned."

Well, there was that. The child had a point. Still . . . "But I didn't, did I?"

"Becca died in the twister." Okay, maybe this wasn't the best game to play to make Katie feel better.

"Yes, but that wasn't anything that happened to us." Immediately Fannie regretted her words. That twister had definitely happened to her little sister. "I'm sorry, Katie. I know you miss Becca."

She nodded. "It's okay."

"But for the most part, God has kept us safe. Right?"

"What about Tom coming back for you, and Kip and me almost having to live with Mrs. Kane?"

Unable to refrain from expelling a frustrated breath, Fannie shrugged in defeat.

"I don't know, Katie. All those bad things happened. But we made it through. Maybe we shouldn't expect God to keep us from bad things, but pray that He gets us through them instead."

Fannie fell silent. She had so much to learn about God, who was she to try to talk to Katie about what God would or wouldn't keep them safe from?

Thankfully, she was spared the necessity of returning to the no-win conversation by the sound of a bark. More like a bark and a squawk . . . lots of barking, lots of squawking.

Katie's eyes opened wider. "Uh-oh. Mr. Kane's puppy is going to be in big trouble this time."

"Oh, brother. Just what Blake needs right now."

Toni's heart went out to Mrs. Kane as Blake laid down the sentence. The puppy had to go.

Amanda Kane clutched her dog. "We can't just kill him." Unaware of his precarious position, the animal wiggled to get loose.

Blake drew a slow breath and exhaled. "I'm sorry, Mrs. Kane. I know the dog means a lot to you, but the fact is, he's a menace to this wagon train."

"But that's the first time he's gotten loose in two weeks."

Mrs. Kane had a point. The animal had been astonishingly well-behaved lately.

"It don't make no matter." The other voice of the argument. Curtis Adams. "That dog done kilt another of my chickens. If you don't shoot it, I'll kill it myself."

Mr. Kane stepped forward with menacing intention. "You lay one hand on my dog and I won't be held responsible for what I do to ya."

Blake held up his hands and silence ensued. "Listen folks. The matter is easily resolved." He turned to Mr. and Mrs. Kane. "You've been warned time and again. The dog has to go. If you don't have the strength to take care of him, we'll find someone who does. There's no shame in it."

A pitiful sob escaped Mrs. Kane's throat. "Haven't I suffered enough?" She knelt beside her half-grown puppy and buried her face in the course fur. The animal gave a little whine and swiped her face with his tongue.

"I like that dog." All eyes turned to Alfred.

"Be quiet boy," Mr. Harrison snapped.

"Sorry, Pa."

"It's all right, Mr. Harrison. I like the dog too, Alfred," Blake said. "But he got loose again and ate Mr. Adams' chickens."

"It was my fault, Mr. Tanner." Alfred shuffled and looked at the ground, then he cocked his eye toward his pa, clearly trying to decide whether he should risk speaking up again. Apparently, he decided the situation called for a little disobedience, because he squared his thick shoulders and looked at the pup. "I let him go. He don't like being tied up."

Toni's heart went out to the oversized child. He reminded her so much of her little brother, Jacob. Sweet, gentle with animals, kind to all. And really, she couldn't understand why the Adams' chickens couldn't be penned up better. Before she could stop herself, she stepped forward. "Blake. Can I say something?"

Irritation twisted Blake's face. "You might as well."

Ignoring his sarcasm, Toni cleared her throat. "Alfred has a point."

"Thank you, ma'am," the boy said, though he obviously didn't understand what was happening.

"You're welcome." She smiled at him and received an enormous grin in return.

"What are you getting at, Toni?" Blake asked, still failing to conceal his irritation.

"Well, it's just that. The puppy isn't solely to blame here."

Curtis puffed up like a peacock, obviously believing her to be on his side and flattered by the attention. "I'd say not. That dimwit turned him loose." He turned to Mr. Harrison. "You should keep that boy tied up."

Toni gasped. "Mr. Adams, you're a cruel man to even suggest such a thing. Alfred is a sweet young man and he did nothing wrong."

"Thank you, ma'am," Alfred said again, melting Toni's heart.

"You're welcome, Alfred."

"You're nice."

"So are you."

Blake cleared his throat. Loudly. "What is your point, Toni?"

"Just that if Mr. Adams had kept those chickens penned up like the rules of the wagon train clearly state, the dog wouldn't be running after them. There is nothing in the rules that say a dog has to be kept on a rope." She smiled innocently. "Unless I missed that one somewhere?"

Behind her, Ginger snickered. Toni tensed. *Please God, don't let Ginger make this worse by mocking Blake.*

Mr. Kane stood a little straighter. "Come to think of it, the whore's right."

Toni's cheeks burned and suddenly she felt the urge to slink away.

Sam moved next to Toni just as she started to retreat. "Mr. Kane, considering this woman is trying to save your dog, I'd suggest using a little more respect."

"Respect . . . ?"

Ginger stepped forward. "Yeah. She already told you people she wasn't taking that off you any more."

The girl jabbed Toni in the ribs. Toni winced, but she got the message. She couldn't let this man get away with this treatment of her. She squared her shoulders to bolster her resolve. "Yes. I told you before that I will not stand by and be called vile names by you or anyone else. So kindly remember that in the future. Furthermore, Mr. Kane, I'm not reminding Blake of the rules for your sake, but rather your wife's because as she said . . . she's lost enough. She shouldn't have to lose her dog because Mr. Adams is lazy and won't fix his pen properly. Personally, I think we should butcher the rest of them and have fried chicken."

Laughter rose from the crowd. The sound was more welcome to Toni than if they had hired a symphony to play in her honor.

"Toni is right," Miss Sadie said. "That puppy is doing what comes natural to dogs. Mr. Adams should keep the chickens penned up properly and he might make it to Oregon with a few of them." A few more folks spoke up and slowly, consensus shifted from killing the puppy to holding the Adamses responsible for their chickens. Even Mr. Harrison lost his surly expression and his face broke out in a grin.

Alfred patted the pup's head. "It's okay, Wolf, I like chicken too."'

Once again laughter rose from the crowd.

Blake eyed Mr. Adams. "Looks like you know what has to be done. If the puppy gets hold of them because they get loose, it's your own fault. Keep them penned and in your wagon. Or we'll be having us some fried chicken like Toni suggested."

Toni's stomach turned over as she recognized the look of pure venom shooting from Mr. Adams' eyes. "Never thought I'd see the day when a dirty whore called the shots around here. She ain't been nothin' but trouble since the day she and that little redheaded floozy joined."

Blake sprang into action and landed a blow to the man's jaw. He would have joined him on the ground and finished the job, but Sam got to him in time to grab his arm. "Blake! This isn't the way. The man is angry and humiliated. Let him cool off. He will apologize."

Blake pointed at Mr. Adams, who still hadn't quite figured out what hit him. "Get that pen fixed and then join the detail making rafts. And don't let me ever hear you refer to my wife as anything other than the good respectable woman she is. Is that clear?"

The man sneered, but Sam gave him a swift nudge with his moccasin-bound foot. Mr. Adams visibly conceded. He nodded. "Clear."

Sam reached down to help the man to his feet. Mr. Adams spat into the dirt and ignored the hand. "The day I need a breed's help is the day I put a bullet in my head."

"Suit yourself."

As Mr. Adams stomped toward his wagon, Toni expelled the breath she'd been holding throughout the entire exchange. Ginger stomped right up to Sam and frowned, her brows pushed together, causing a deep well between her eyes. "Why did you let him get by with talking to you that way?" she demanded .

Sam smiled at her, and Toni wondered if he was thinking the same thing. That only a couple of weeks ago, Ginger, herself had referred to him as "breed." "If we only forgive those who ask for forgiveness, we're no better than those who don't know Jesus."

Ginger rolled her eyes. "It's always about God with you, isn't it?"

With a wink, he nodded. "Almost always, I must admit."

His gaze shifted from Ginger to Toni. She smiled at him. Sam, without his Bible talk just wouldn't be right.

Ginger gave a "hrmph." "You two make me sick." With that she stomped off.

Sam shook his head as he stared after her. "She doesn't much care for any talk about God, does she?"

"Not much," Toni murmured.

Sam obviously thought Ginger's huffy exit was a result of his unapologetic talk about God. But Toni had a feeling Ginger thought the smile Toni had shared with Sam meant more than friendship.

If only she were right.

Eleven

The next day's crossing of the Platte just before the Red Buttes went smoothly and without incident. Much to everyone's relief, Toni's included. At the end of a long day of crossing, it was a mercy to sit by a warm campfire and listen to the sounds of the night. Not only the sounds of nature. But Toni had grown accustomed to listening to families preparing for bed. Children being read Bible stories or told stories from the imaginations of their parents. The cattle lowed in the circle, the sound almost soothing her to sleep as she rested her back against a wagon wheel.

Ginger had taken a group of women to the river for baths. Toni would go later. She still couldn't bring herself to disrobe in front of "respectable" women. Ginger was as tough-talking and clear-shooting as any man, so she had become the protector when the men couldn't be around. Which, in this case, they obviously couldn't.

The quiet filled her with contentment. After two weeks with no threat from the Indians, she was beginning to feel confident that maybe Swooping Eagle had decided she was more trouble than she was worth. Still, she didn't take any chances these days. Not only did she pin her hair up; she also covered it with a loose shawl.

"Mind a little company, Toni?"

Toni looked into the still attractive face of Sadie Barnes. The wagon train matriarch had always been kind to Fannie and Toni and she couldn't help but welcome her into the solitude.

"Nothing would give me more pleasure, Miss Sadie."

The woman grunted as she lowered herself to the ground next to Toni. She settled against the other half of the wheel. "You might have to help me back up." She chuckled.

"I'd be happy to. If you can't manage."

"You did a good thing with that puppy."

A flush of pleasure drifted across Toni's face. "Thank you, ma'am."

"That Harrison boy is sweet as he can be, isn't he?"

Toni smiled. "He is. I wish I could find a prairie chicken to kill and fry for him."

"His mother doted on him. He must be devastated without her."

"You'd never know it. He seems happy."

"People like that bury their pain. He's simple, but he's not stupid or without feelings. He's confused and doesn't know what to think of his ma being gone. He needs a good ma."

"Yes, I suppose he does."

"Mr. Harrison's probably going to be looking for a wife soon."

A gasp left Toni's throat. "Mrs. Harrison is barely cold in the grave."

Miss Sadie nodded. "Men rarely marry for love, Toni. He has a simple boy and a daughter on the verge of womanhood. He needs a real woman to help him make sense of everything."

"Well, best of luck to him."

"You could do worse, young lady."

Toni whipped around and stared into wizened old eyes. "Me? What do you mean?"

Miss Sadie gave a shrug of plump but sturdy shoulders. "Mr. Harrison is a little rough around the edges, but he made his money back east in a string of hotels. Anyone who marries him will want for nothing."

Suddenly, the warm night felt chilled. Toni found her voice with difficulty. "Do you hear what you're suggesting?" For the first time in the months she'd known Miss Sadie, Toni disliked the older woman immensely.

"Merely that you stop being so picky and find yourself a decent man to marry. It's not likely a woman such as yourself will have too many opportunities and at least you like the boy. Most women would have him institutionalized."

Toni straightened her shoulders, never feeling the weight of her former profession more strongly than she did this second. "You are suggesting I sell myself in marriage to a man I do not love because he has money and I will never find someone to love me."

"I didn't mean to offend." Miss Sadie patted Toni's leg. "Maybe you are good enough for Sam after all."

"Good enough for Sam? What do you mean? What have you heard, Miss Sadie?"

"Relax. I haven't heard anything. I only know what I observe and unless I miss my guess, you are smitten with our wagon scout."

Grateful for the cover of darkness to hide her flaming cheeks, Toni cleared her throat. "You're mistaken, ma'am. I don't intend to marry. Not Mr. Harrison. Not Sam."

"Indeed? And what is a woman alone planning to do?"

Toni's lips lifted in a grin. "You should know, shouldn't you? What are your plans?"

"It's not the same for you as it is for me. I've lived my life, borne and lost my sons and now I'm going west to die. I'll hire myself a small log home built. I'll raise chickens and a cow or two. I'll fish in the river and plant a garden."

"That sounds lovely, Miss Sadie. I believe I'll do the same thing." And it did sound lovely.

"No. That's not a life for a woman like you."

Toni bristled. "What exactly do you mean?"

"Simmer down. You surely do have a temper, don't you?"

"I didn't know I did, but I guess maybe I do."

"What I meant was a woman with so much love to give shouldn't be alone."

Still not completely mollified, Toni stared closer at the older woman. "And by having a lot of love to give, you mean . . ."

"You should be a mother. Have half a dozen young'uns, dogs, goats, chickens, cows. All manner of cuddly things you can pour out that generous soul to."

Toni gave a short laugh. "You forgot one not-so-small detail, Miss Sadie."

"Oh?"

"In order for me to have all those cuddly things in my life, wouldn't I first need a husband?"

"Now you're seeing reason." The woman's eyes twinkled and Toni finally figured out that she'd been had.

She laughed and slipped an arm around Miss Sadie. "Some of us are meant to be mothers. Some of us are meant to be kind to other women's children. I think the second category is where I fit."

"If that's where you fall, so be it. But don't close your mind to the possibility of God bringing love your way. Sam, for instance."

Toni's heart leapt at the thought. "Sam has better things on his mind than worrying about a spinster, former prostitute setting her cap for him. I respect him too much to put him in that position."

"He could do worse."

The praise lit a candle inside of Toni and she knew she must be glowing. "Thank you, Miss Sadie. He might could do worse, but he could also most definitely do much better. I wouldn't take that chance away from him."

The sound of crashing footsteps caused Toni to shoot to her feet.

"I swear!" Ginger sloshed into camp and sat, yanking her moccasins off.

"Ginger! You scared me half to death. What happened?"

Toni asked, trying to hide a grin as she looked over the girl's bedraggled appearance.

"Those women," she sputtered. "That's the last time I protect them while they take a bath."

"For goodness sakes, are you going to tell me what happened, or aren't you?"

"Ain't it obvious?" she grabbed her braid and began wringing water.

"You fell in the river?" Miss Sadie ventured a guess.

"Ha!" Ginger continued wringing out her long braid that hung down past the curve of her waist. "Those ungrateful, mean-spirited women ganged up on me and derned if they didn't throw me right in."

Toni burst into peals of merry laughter. "Serves you right. When was the last time you had a bath?" When she'd given Ginger the new clothes, she'd had high hopes the young woman would continue to exhibit good bathing habits. But the opposite had proven true. And apparently she wasn't the only one getting tired of it.

"I just had one two weeks ago!"

"Most women will take one at any given opportunity. Don't you want to smell nice?"

"You sayin' I don't?" Ginger's brow puckered in anger.

That was an extremely loaded question. Toni searched for a way around it without being blunt. "I'm saying anyone who doesn't take a bath on a regular basis or at the very least use a cloth and wash up, is going to give off a certain unpleasant odor."

"I don't believe it. I just plumb don't believe it. You *do* think I stink."

"Simmer down," Miss Sadie said. "Come here, young lady. Help me get up."

Whether she was too stunned to refuse or just didn't know what to say, Ginger sloshed over to where the older woman sat and extended her hand.

"Thank you."

"You're welcome," Ginger mumbled.

"May I?" Miss Sadie asked, grasping Ginger's arm.

"What are you gonna do?"

Toni had to admit, she too was intrigued.

"You'll see." Lickety split, Miss Sadie raised Ginger's arm. "Take a whiff."

Even Toni, who thought she'd seen everything there was to see, was shocked. Ginger's face blanched for a second and then turned scarlet. "There ain't no sense insulting me."

"Now listen." Miss Sadie let go of Ginger's wrist. "No one is trying to insult you, but for a lovely young woman, such as yourself, to walk around dirty and smelling offensively when there is a perfectly good body of water right next to us, is shameful. There is no excuse, if you want to be decent and respectable."

"Well . . ."

Toni peered closer, taking in the first sight of vulnerability in Ginger. Was her lip actually trembling? "I-I gotta go do somethin'."

With that, Ginger stomped away.

"Well," Toni said with a sigh. "At least you tried, Miss Sadie. May I walk you back to your wagon?"

Miss Sadie smiled. "I might be on in years, but I can carry myself home. Thank you, though. You're a good girl."

Toni watched the widow walk toward her own wagon. Miss Sadie was right. She had already lived her life with a husband and children, so the thought of spending the rest of her days alone didn't seem like such a tragedy.

Regret twisted inside Toni. Regret that she would never marry and raise children of her own. The pain was almost unbearable.

"Please, Lord," she whispered. "Help me be content to walk the road you've laid out for me." But the road seemed so long, so winding, and so steep, she wondered how on earth she would ever endure.

Sleep eluded Sam as unease filled him. It was difficult to decide whether or not he was sensing danger—such as from Swooping Eagle. Or whether the tension in the train between those who thought the dog should go and those who thought the chickens should be penned was merely worrying him more than necessary.

A howl in the distance jolted him upward. He listened again. Another howl. Standing, he placed his hand on his gun. Blake stood next to the wagon he now shared with his wife.

"You heard?" Sam asked, walking the few feet from his bedroll to the wagon.

Blake nodded.

"Think it could be Swooping Eagle?"

"Could be. In any case, we can rule out wolves for that howling."

Sam nodded. "We best keep extra guards on the women tonight."

"Agreed."

"I'll see to it."

As though by instinct, Sam turned toward Toni's wagon. A shadow passed around the canvas on the outside of the wagon. His stomach turned. He crept close, careful to stay out of the light of the campfires so that he didn't cast his own shadow.

It wasn't probable Swooping Eagle would launch another attack such as the one he'd already lost. But to send in warriors in twos or threes to kidnap his original target was highly likely and something Sam had been anticipating. He only wondered why it had taken the chief this long. He must have been wounded worse than Sam thought.

He continued his stealthy pursuit until he reached the wagon. The shadow was walking away from the wagon, not toward it. That could only mean one thing. The Cheyenne chief was no longer interested in kidnapping. Revenge was on his mind. Sam tried to swallow along a dry throat as fear gripped him. The thought of anyone harming Toni filled him with terror, but he knew he couldn't act rashly. *Please, Lord. She's been through so much already. Don't let our enemy win over us.* He moved quietly, but quickly, determined to do whatever it took to help the Almighty keep Toni safe.

Twelve

Toni woke with a start and sat up with the uneasy feeling something wasn't right. Instinct, born of years of having to look out for herself, shot through her and she scanned the darkened wagon searching for anything that might be out of place.

One thing in particular caught her attention. Where was Ginger? The girl knew better than to go off alone. Especially at night. Toni moved stealthily through the wagon until she reached the opening in the canvas, pulled it aside, and slipped her head and shoulders out. "Ginger!" she hissed.

A hand clapped over her mouth. Toni's muffled scream tore through her throat as she was pulled through the wagon opening and landed almost gently on her feet. The hand remained firmly in place while another arm kept her firmly caged against a rock-hard body. Toni fought against the contracting muscles of her captor's arm.

"Shh. Toni!" Hot breath wisped her hair against her ear. "It's Sam."

White relief flowed over her and she leaned back against his warm chest. Strong arms encircled her from behind. "It's all right," he whispered. "Do not be afraid. I am taking my hand away."

"Sam, for Mercy's sake." Toni turned in his arms as relief gave way to quandary. "Why did you pull me out of the wagon that way? I thought you were trying to kidnap me." She swatted his chest with the back of her hand.

Sam covered her hand, then held it. "I'm sorry. It was the fastest way I knew to keep you from screaming." He kept his voice low. "I saw someone walking from your wagon."

Keenly aware of her hand tucked inside of Sam's, Toni slipped her fingers free. There were too many emotions swirling around her chest and no time to think about what they meant.

"Ginger's missing," she said. "Maybe she's the one you saw."

Sam nodded. "Probably. But I had better go find out." He expelled a heavy breath. "No one is supposed to leave camp. So if she wasn't taken against her will, she will have some explaining to do."

"I agree. It's difficult to tell Ginger anything."

"You'd best climb back inside while I go look for her."

Toni shook her head. "I'm coming with you."

Sam stopped and turned. "I don't think that's a good idea. You would be safer here in the circle of the wagons."

Toni couldn't deny the earnestness in Sam's eyes, but she couldn't quite believe she'd be safer if she stayed at the wagon. As a matter of fact, she never felt more protected than when she was with Sam. Of course she'd never admit it. But she still didn't enjoy the thought of staying behind while Sam wandered off through the dark to find Ginger.

"I'm going."

Sam paused. "All right. Stay close."

Sam knew there were more people in the woods than Ginger, Toni, and himself. Ginger was most definitely speaking with someone. And thirty yards away, someone else listened just the same as he and Toni were doing. That worried him a little. Of course, he knew they weren't Indians. Cheyenne warriors wouldn't be so obvious. So that was good news. But the threat of outlaws was still a genuine concern.

He placed his finger to his lips. Toni nodded. Her quiet acceptance never failed to speak to him and give him confidence in her wisdom. He moved one step forward, but at the sound of a splash, he picked up his steps and rushed toward the river, with Toni close on his heels. They entered the clearing the same time as Grant Kelley. "What's going on?"

"The girl's having a much needed bath." The three of them whipped about at the same time to find Miss Sadie standing against a tree, holding a pile of clothes.

"Miss Sadie!" Sam felt the indignation to his core. "What in thunderation are you doing out here? You know the rules."

"Hogwash." She said with a snort. "Rules don't apply to me."

"I wonder what Blake would say about that," Grant spoke up.

"Are you okay, Miss Sadie? Who's with you?" Ginger called from the water.

"I'm all right, hon. It's just Sam, Mr. Kelley, and Toni. I'm guessing they were worried about you. I told you you shouldn't have gone off alone."

"Toni! You shouldn't be out here. Them redskins could be back any minute."

"You don't have to worry. I'm with Sam."

Irritation fled at her simple statement. This woman . . . Sam knew for the first time someone had come into his life with the capacity to break his heart. He also had no doubt that heartbreak was the only outcome for him if he allowed himself to think with a white man's heart. Because the truth of the matter was that he wasn't a white man. Not completely. And the half of him that carried Sioux blood was the half that the world would never allow to be with a woman like Toni Rodden.

Lord, guard my heart. Don't let me move out of my own desires. Please help me to keep what's best for Toni in mind.

Even if that meant he had to let her go. His next prayer beseeched God for strength to do just that. But only if there was no other way.

Toni's body ached as the wagon flung her all over the wagon seat. Ginger had actually talked Blake into allowing her to join the scouts, so once again Toni was back to doing all the driving. For the last three days, she'd had no respite from the endless beating her body got from wrestling with the oxen in the deep-rutted road that was gradually, but visibly ascending.

Worse still, her wagon had fallen toward the end of the line in rotation and she couldn't see Sam as he rode along with Blake toward the front of the line. When commotion ahead caught her attention, she welcomed the change in scenery. "What is it?" she called to Amanda Kane, who walked close by. The woman had practically been connected to Toni since she saved the half-wolf pup.

"Looks like wagons are coming this way."

"Coming? Like turning back? Why on earth . . . ?"

Amanda gave a lift of her too-thin shoulders. "It would appear so. Wolfie, stay!" Surprisingly, the puppy inched faithfully back to her side. Happy to be off the rope. As though he knew he'd had a close call, he had been getting into less trouble since the last chicken incident. "How did you get him to obey?" Toni asked, as curiosity got the better of her.

Mrs. Kane grinned. "Alfie."

"Alfie?"

"Alfred Harrison. He's a wonder with animals." Mrs. Kane's face held a softness Toni hadn't noticed in the woman since before Becca's death.

"He's a special young man, isn't he?"

She smiled and nodded, then her face clouded over. "I wish his own pa could see that. The man barely even notices he has children."

The fact wasn't news to Toni. Or anyone who had paid attention. "Mr. Harrison isn't mean to him, is he?"

"Oh, no. Doesn't seem to be. Mainly he ignores those children. Both of them. I reckon he's too grieved to know how to take care of them. You know their ma did all of the looking after them before she was killed." She stared off across the horizon. "If they were mine . . ." Her expression dropped and she jerked her chin quickly before Toni could respond. "Oh, look. Blake's calling a halt so he can talk to the other wagon."

Toni made a mental note to pray harder for Amanda. The poor woman had endured more than any human being should have to endure in two lifetimes let alone one short life.

Sam and Blake spoke with someone who appeared to be the leader of the other group of travelers for at least twenty minutes, and at the end of their discussion the trains maneuvered into one large circle.

Toni climbed down from the wagon and stretched her back. Finding little relief, she went straight to work. No sense putting off the difficult task of unhooking the oxen and setting them loose to graze in the center of the wagon circle.

The oxen had been noticeably slower. Partly, Toni knew, due to the ascent of the train. But also, the rocky terrain bruised their feet so going was slower than it had been on the grassy plains of Kansas and the land before Fort Laramie.

She bent to unharness the oxen from the wagon. Her hands still hadn't callused back over completely and the blisters of the early days on the trail were re-forming, causing burning, raw sores on her palms and fingers.

She straightened to find a grinning Alfred standing in front of the oxen. Whispering and patting one of the enormous beasts as though it was no larger than a puppy, Alfred actually seemed to understand the animals.

"How are you, Alfred?"

"Good. I like ox."

"You do?" Toni patted the lad's shoulder as she walked around him to remove the yoke.

He nodded. "I'll do it."

"It's okay, Alfred. You don't have to."

His face clouded with disappointment. "Yes, ma'am," he mumbled, still staring at the oxen.

"You want to?" Toni asked.

Brown eyes lit and he nodded.

"All right. If you're sure."

In minutes, the boy had turned the oxen out to graze. He lifted his arm to her and waved his goodbye.

"Thanks again, Alfred."

"Okay, bye."

Ginger arrived riding astride a large, black mare named Tulip. The horse was cantankerous and stubborn—a perfect match for Ginger as far as Toni was concerned.

"Dadburn horse," the girl muttered as she reined in with difficulty and dismounted. "I ought to shoot it and get me another one."

Toni smiled. As much as Ginger complained, she loved that animal as much as Alfred loved Wolf and she'd defend it within an inch of her own life.

"So what's going on up there?" Toni asked. If anyone would know, Ginger would have found a way to worm the information out of Sam or Blake.

Ginger jerked her thumb toward the other wagon. "Your Indian."

"Sam?"

Ginger's face went blank, then her lips twisted into a wry grin. "Sam's *your* Indian?"

Realizing her mistake, Toni felt the humiliation to her toes. "Of course not. Don't be ridiculous. What do you mean *my Indian?*"

"The other train was attacked by the Cheyenne a few days ago."

Toni's heart nearly stopped. No wonder things had been so quiet from Swooping Eagle. He had moved on to wreak havoc with another group of travelers.

"How much damage did he do?"

Ginger shook her head, looping Tulip's reins around the wagon tongue. "Bad. Twenty wagons were burned and eight men were killed. They took one woman and four young'uns."

Toni drew in a sharp breath. That might have been her if Swooping Eagle had had his way. She envisioned the poor woman and children. They must be terrified. Were they being treated well? She shuddered as all kinds of images came to mind.

"Anyway," Ginger continued. "The good news for us, according to Sam, is that those Indians are more than likely going to take their captives to their village. So we won't have to worry about attack for awhile."

"Is anyone going after the captives?"

"I think some of the men from the other train are discussing that with Blake."

Toni scanned the circle until she spotted Sam. He and

Blake were in deep conversation with the leader of the other wagon train and, as Ginger mentioned, several other men. Some spoke calmly, others with noticeable agitation. Her heart picked up a beat. What if Sam decided to join a search party? Blake couldn't go. As the wagon master, his place was firmly with the wagon train. So Sam seemed the next logical person to help. He knew this country, after years of scouting for several trains.

Toni nodded as though answering her own question. "Sam's going to go with them."

Ginger followed her gaze. "Yep. Probably."

"What if he gets hurt?"

"That's his choice."

"But . . ."

"But what, Toni? All you have to do is ask him not to go and he'd stay. The man loves you. Don't you know that?"

"Oh, Ginger. You haven't known Sam very long. He loves everyone. He's much the way I imagine Jesus must have been when he was alive."

"Oh, for the love o . . ." Ginger snorted and twisted her face into a scowl. "He's a nice man, for sure, but he's not exactly the Almighty."

"No, he's not." Toni smiled. "But he's the closest thing I've ever seen in a human being."

"Mercy, you really do love him, don't you?"

Toni kept her gaze fixed on Sam. Her shoulders rose and fell in a heavy breath. "What is love?" she whispered. "If I did love him, how would I know?"

Thirteen

"I say we stay on the trail headin' back. We'll ask for help once we get to Fort Laramie." The leader of the second wagon train had been trying to force his opinion, and for a time it seemed as though his tactic would work. For the last few minutes he'd repeated his argument over and over, generally trying to wear down the grieving members of his train. "We need soldiers to help us find the woman and girls. There's no choice. We go back." He spat a stream of tobacco juice as though that settled things.

"And leave my little girl at the mercy of those savages for two more weeks?" Timothy Franks, a middle-aged man from Kansas, spoke with the passion of a father desperate to retrieve his child. "Those murdering redskins killed my wife. Janey is all I have left."

Sam listened to the argument between the members of the new wagon train with growing impatience. The former wagon master had been among the first to take an arrow through the heart. In his absence an overbearing former mountain man by the name of Joseph Thompson had declared himself the leader of the group. Of the remaining men, he seemed the strongest. The loudest at the very least. Sam knew from experience that too often anyone who made the most noise ended up at the front of the line.

"Now, listen." Blake raised his hands for silence. "I can't tell you all what to do. Anyone with a wagon of your own and enough supplies to make it to Oregon is free to join us. The rest of you will have to take a vote to decide if you go after the captives or stay on the trail back east."

"Can't you spare some men to help with a search?" Brian Stamm, a young farmer from Minnesota spoke up. "Angela is my sister. I promised my ma I'd take care of her. That's the only reason my pa and ma let her come with my wife and me." His voice cracked with emotion. "I failed them."

Sam's heart went out to the man when Blake shook his head. "I'm sorry about your sister and I'd like to help, but we lost 150 members ourselves a few months back. I can't risk the strength of my wagon train by organizing a search party. We have to protect the wagons, supplies, and women and children in our own train." Sam knew Blake was right. But he also knew that if Toni had been captured, he would have left regardless, and no one would have been able to force him to remain with the wagon train. He also understood Blake's position and couldn't blame him.

Blake's tone remained calm as he tried to explain further. "Swooping Eagle could be planning an attack on us next. We can't spare any men. At least not enough to make a difference should you engage the Indians in battle."

The man's countenance fell at the disappointing news. Then his jaw tightened with determination. "I'm going on my own."

The new wagon master from the other train stepped forward, towering over the distraught brother. "No one's leaving this train. Just like Mr. Tanner, here, we need every man in case of another attack."

Sam's defenses rose at this man's audacity.

"Excuse me, sir," he said. "Mr. Tanner has already agreed to take on anyone who wants to join our train. So you can't exactly keep people prisoner in your wagon train."

Anger flashed in the man's eyes. "I can do whatever I want. I took over after our leader got an arrow through his heart. They wanted me to be their leader and I'll be hanged if I'm going to take a chance on losing any more lives just because a couple of people want to go on a fool's errand."

"Fool's errand?" Timothy Franks stepped forward, anger flashing in his eyes. "I don't consider looking for my daughter to be a fool's errand. I'm going with Brian. And if anyone's a fool here, it's you. 'Specially if you think you're going to keep me from going after my little girl."

"You challenging me?" Joseph's eyes took on a dangerous glare as he stared down at the determined father.

Sam planted his feet, poised to jump in if he needed to do so.

Brian and Timothy made an impressive wall of strength as they stood shoulder to shoulder against a man who could more than likely kill them both with his bare hands. "I'm challenging your right to keep a man from taking care of his own." Timothy stared him in the eye. "My little girl needs me. I never should have agreed to turn tail and run back to the fort in the first place."

"Now you callin' me a coward?"

"Nope. I'm saying it was a mistake not to go right after those Indians when their trail was fresh and they were still close enough to catch up to. I don't know how we'll ever find them now. But with God's help, I aim to try."

"Same here," Brian said. "Don't even try to stop me."

"If you go, don't come crawlin' back. You won't be welcome in our train."

"Don't worry. I can get my little girl back to Minnesota on my own, just fine. I wouldn't want to ride with the likes of you, anyhow."

Brian turned to Blake. "If it's all the same to you, I'd appreciate a spot in your wagon train for my wife and son while I look for my sister." His lip curled and he cast a glance at Joseph. "I wouldn't trust this man to keep them safe."

Blake nodded. "Our general rule is not to take women traveling without a man, but we've broken it a couple of times. I guess this is good enough reason as any."

Brian clasped and shook Blake's hand. "Thank you. You won't regret it."

Sam stepped forward. He knew they couldn't send these men out as sheep among wolves. Two farmers from the plains, they wouldn't survive a week alone. "You'll need a tracker."

Feeling Blake's gaze boring into him, Sam kept his focus on the two men.

"You offering to help?"

"He can't," Blake said, anger edging his voice. "He has a contract with this wagon train company. If he leaves he won't receive his pay for this trip."

A smile tipped Sam's lips. Blake was speaking from fear, nothing more. "Sometimes doing the right thing costs. Just ask Jesus. His cost was much higher than losing a few months' wages."

Scowling deeply, Blake turned silently on his heel and stomped away.

Sam understood his friend's concerns. He didn't want to go off from the wagon train, either. For one thing, he hated the thought of leaving Toni without a protector, but this was the right decision for more than one reason. First of all, if Swooping Eagle was in camp, he was no immediate threat to Toni. Second, only meeting the war chief face-to-face would give Sam the answers he sought. A man as powerful as this Cheyenne wouldn't pursue a strange woman for no reason. Sam was determined to discover the truth. One way or another he would end this man's threat against Toni.

Typically, when a wagon train met up with other travelers there was cause for a celebration. A full day of camp, a feast if they could find game, and stories around the fire, music, or Bible studies. But this was no time to celebrate. The eastbound train had suffered too much and there were very few smiles to be had.

Neither did Toni feel like celebrating. As a matter of fact, she was downright angry at the thought of Sam riding off with two strangers, risking his life on what was surely a futile search.

He stood before her now as she prepared supper for herself and Ginger. Her spoon clattered in the pot as she stirred the beans with more vigor than necessary. "Toni, why are you angry with me?" His voice rang with sorrow.

"What makes you think I'm angry?" Toni gave a nonchalant wave and resumed her stirring.

The soft warmth of Sam's hand upon her shoulder stopped her pretense. "Fine," she said, facing him. "I am angry. You shouldn't be risking your neck for a couple of strangers."

"But this is what I feel is the right thing for me to do." A gentle smile curved his lips. "Would you have me deny what I feel inside?"

Toni scowled at him, drums of defeat playing against her chest. "No. I just wish you'd feel something a little more intelligent."

Sam laughed, "Toni, I've tracked this land for over fifteen years. I know the ways of the Cheyenne as well as the other plains Indians. If God can use anyone to lead those two men to find their loved ones, it is I."

"Why can't they just go back to Fort Laramie and ask for a search party?" Toni knew her manner was that of a spoiled child, but she didn't care. She truly didn't. All she knew was that Sam was leaving.

Taking a long, slow breath, Sam clasped her other shoulder and looked down, his eyes filled with tenderness. "I am honored by your concern."

Toni could barely breathe when he looked at her that way. The way a man did when he wanted more than an hour with a woman. She swallowed hard and stepped back, overwhelmed by the emotions welling inside of her. "When are you leaving?" she said, barely above a whisper.

He dropped his hands from her shoulders, but continued to stare at her . . . searching, asking. . . . something. "First light."

Toni wanted to say so many things. Things like: Be careful, come back to me, love me. But she knew better. Now wasn't the time to ask for anything or make any emotional statements. Or maybe it was. Maybe. "Sam . . ."

"Tarnation, Toni! You sending up smoke signals or something?"

Toni jumped at the sound of Ginger's outraged voice. Once her words hit their mark, Toni gasped. "Mercy!" Springing into action she dashed for the pot. Black smoke billowed into the air and the acrid smell burned her throat. "I've never burned a pot of anything in my whole life."

"Why'd you have to go and start now?" Ginger grumbled. "I'm hungry as a bear."

Sam reached for the handle of the pot and removed it from the fire. "Come with me."

"Where to?" Toni asked.

"The river." He smiled. "I'll catch some fish for your supper, while you use pebbles to scrub the pot."

Ginger's scowl said it all. She wasn't about to wait for food, nor was she going to help scrub a pot. "I'm goin' to find out what Miss Sadie's fixin'. She probably has enough to invite me to join her."

Toni sent her a look of apology. "I promise I won't burn tomorrow's supper."

The young woman waved aside the apology. "Don't worry. I won't go hungry." She glanced at Sam. "Hopefully you won't either."

Toni followed Sam to the river. She felt awkward and unsure of herself. How could she have come so close to saying words she would most certainly regret? Thank heavens Ginger had interrupted when she had.

But what if Sam didn't return? The thought of him lying on the ground with an arrow through his chest was a possible reality that was too much for her.

"Sam."

The scout turned. "Everything okay?"

"No." She stepped closer to him. "No, Sam, everything is not okay."

He frowned and looked her over. "You hurt?"

She took his hand and pressed a kiss to each of his callused fingers. "The only pain I feel is in my heart, at the thought of you leaving."

Sam dropped the pot on the ground by his feet. Gently, he pulled his hand from her grip. "Toni, this isn't proper."

A short laugh erupted from Toni. "Proper? Do you think I don't know what is and is not proper?"

"I don't mean to insult you. Forgive me."

His humble reply took the thunder from her. "Oh, Sam. Proper is a matter of interpretation. I behaved in the proper manner for my situation. Entertaining was the only way I knew to get my life back. A real life. I know I'll always have the mark of a prostitute on me. And I know that these people are never going to accept me in proper society. But I don't care about any of that. Not anymore. What I care about is you. I know you won't love me. But I wanted you to know how I feel before you go."

Her lungs burned by the time she finished her speech and she realized she'd given it all in one breath. Her chest rose and fell as she tried to gather air back into her body. "Toni," he said softly stepping closer.

Joy shot through Toni as he pulled her to him.

His eyes scanned her face, coming to rest on her lips. "You're beautiful."

The look in his eyes said he was telling the truth. But his words reminded Toni that she wasn't the woman she'd been before George's attack. "I forget about my scars, both inside and out, when you look at me," she murmured, more as a revelation to herself.

"Nothing could take away your beauty."

"Don't lie to me, Sam." Toni lowered her gaze. "You have no reason to do so."

He placed his finger beneath her chin and forced her eyes upward once again. "You know I do not lie. I have always seen you as beautiful. Inside and out." He drew a deep breath and moved his hand from her chin until his palm came to rest on her cheek. Toni closed her eyes, reveling in the gentle, soothing warmth.

"If I could offer you a life, I would take you as my wife," he said. Toni's eyes popped open.

"Marriage?" Hope beat a rapid rhythm in her chest until

she realized what he had actually said. "Of course not. You couldn't marry me."

His face dropped with a sadness that reflected her own heart. "No. It isn't possible."

On impulse, Toni reached up and grazed his cheek with her fingertips. "You're a good man. I wish you all the happiness you deserve."

"As I do you." In an instant, Toni knew he wouldn't resist his desire to kiss her this time.

Toni barely had the presence of mind to breathe as Sam lowered his head. His warm lips met hers in the first kiss she'd ever received that didn't make her feel broken.

Fourteen

Dawn broke two full hours after Sam, Brian, and Timothy mounted their horses and headed toward the spot where the wagon train had been attacked four days earlier. From there, they'd try to pick up the Indians' trail.

Sam tried to put Toni's kiss from his mind, but found it difficult, even during this time when he needed full utilization of his senses. In his heart, he knew he shouldn't have succumbed to the heady feeling of having her in his arms, having her tell him how she cared for him. At the same time, she knew they couldn't be together. She understood that his Indian blood prevented a match between them. He respected her acceptance of the situation. Most women would have argued and begged and tried to change his mind.

He was, foolishly, a little disappointed that she hadn't.

The wagon train would be a few hours behind them but would grow farther and farther behind as the terrain grew more difficult, the journey more arduous. Men on horseback could make the journey twice as fast as a wagon train.

"My Janey loved every minute of the travel. She loved bein' outside more than anything. It was all her ma could do to keep her from tearin' her little dresses and comin' home from the river all muddied. But she always had a string of fish to show for the mess. Her ma always forgave her and fried the fish up just right. I never should have brought them out here. Never. We was doin' fine on our farm. But I wanted to find gold and dress my girls in the finest silk. Watch them eat fancy meals off fine china. This is all my fault." Timothy couldn't seem to stop talking about his girl. The man was heartbroken over the loss of his wife. And desperate . . . more than desperate to find his child. The level of desperation concerned Sam. When the time came, would Timothy have the presence of mind to hold back while Sam negotiated?

Brian was a hotheaded young man with the passions of youth still burning in his veins. But he'd do what it took to get his sister back without compromising the mission, if Sam was any judge of character. And he surely hoped he was. Given a choice between the two, he'd trust Brian to keep a clear head and steady hand in an emergency.

The early morning air held a chill that sliced Sam's gut. It looked like winter might come early this year. The wagon train had already lost so much time between mishaps and Toni and Fannie's kidnapping, and days here and there for repair and the need to hunt. They were usually almost over the mountains by now, almost to the promised land. But this time they had no less than two or three months' of travel ahead of them. And that was provided there were no more setbacks.

"First thing I'm gonna do when I get my sister back is send her straight home to our ma where she belongs."

"She can go back with Janey and me."

"You're really not going on to Oregon?" Brian stared at the man as though he'd taken leave of his senses. "You're so close. I thought all that talk back there was just to show Joseph you didn't need him."

Tim shook his head. "I'm taking my little girl and I'm goin' back to Minnesota where we belong. Back to my wife's people." He pulled out a handkerchief and swiped it across his nose. "I promised my wife over her grave that I'd take her little girl back home. And that's what I aim to do."

Sam hoped Timothy had the opportunity to keep that promise. And if God would remain merciful, both of these men would find what they were looking for.

"Stop kicking up so much dust, Ginger." Toni's nerves were so taut she felt like screaming.

"You're as snarly as an ol' bear!" Ginger barked back. "Don't take it out on me just because you're missing Sam. You've been moping around for three days. Is this how it's gonna be until he gets back?"

"This has nothing to do with Sam. I'm snarly as an old bear because you're choking me half to death. Go ride ahead."

Ginger scowled and gave a huff. "That's the thanks I get for trying to keep you from getting too lonesome for that half-breed."

Anger shot through Toni. She turned on Ginger. "I'm sick of you calling him that. He might be part Indian, but he's a good man, the best man in the whole world. And if I was almost good enough for him, I'd marry him in half a second."

"Good enough for *him*?" Ginger's eyes narrowed. "Who says you ain't good enough for him?"

"He does." She braced her feet against the wagon floor and tried to keep her seat as the wagon swayed against the deep ruts in the trail.

"That's hogwash and you know it." Two deep lines appeared between Ginger's eyes. "I've half a mind to go after him just to knock some sense into that thick head of his."

"Don't be ridiculous. Besides, it's not hogwash," she said pointedly. "And anyone with any brains knows it."

"I ain't stayin' around here for you to insult me."

"Good," Toni groused, "I'm sick of choking on your dust anyway."

Red with anger, Ginger rode away. Toni's gut twinged with just a touch of guilt. The girl meant well, she knew. But for now, Toni was better off alone with her thoughts and bad mood.

Besides, it took all of her concentration to keep the oxen headed in the right direction. Their feet hurt from the rocks. She knew that and felt sorry for the beasts. Not only did the rocks bruise their feet, but they were forced to pull uphill. According to Blake, they'd be lucky to do five miles a day during this stretch of trail. Tensions were high and old feuds were returning to drive everyone crazy.

To compound things, Wolfie had been caught eating another chicken this very morning. But this time the intelligent pup had somehow gotten through the crate himself. So it truly was his fault and Amanda Kane had had a look of sheer terror on her face ever since the camp awoke and discovered the bloody, feathery mess. She tied Wolf to the wagon, but even Toni doubted that would be good enough now. The pup had been given too many chances.

At dusk, Blake called a halt for the day. Alfred appeared to take care of the oxen as he had each day, like clockwork. In the morning, he hitched the team for her; at the end of the day, he unhitched the team and set them out to graze. His sweet, cheerful countenance never failed to lift her spirits. Only tonight he went about his task with noticeably less gusto than usual.

"What's the matter, Alfred?"

He shrugged and shook his head woefully. "I like that dog."

Compassion squeezed Toni's heart. "I know you do. Wolf's a nice puppy. But he has to learn to be good. Doesn't he?"

"He's a good dog."

"Good dogs don't steal chickens."

"Wolf don't do that no more." Alfred gave a deep sigh. "I taught him not to be bad."

"But Alfred, remember Mr. and Mrs. Adams had the chickens?"

"Yes, ma'am."

"Well, this morning they found one of the crates broken into and their last rooster dead."

Alfred shook his head. "Wolf didn't do it. He just ate it. He didn't kill it."

Toni smiled at the lad. He obviously couldn't bear the thought of his friend being accused. And she didn't blame him. "Well, maybe not."

"Yeah. Maybe not." Alfred's face lit. "Mr. Kane was nice to give the rooster to him, huh?"

"No, sweetheart. He didn't give the rooster to Wolfie. The dog took it from the crate."

"I saw it."

"Saw what Alfred?" Toni's mind tried to wrap around what Alfred was saying. But something told her the puppy might have been framed for a murder he didn't commit. She dropped her tone considerably and leaned ever so slightly toward the boy. "Did you see Mr. Kane give the chicken to Wolf?"

Alfred nodded in simple innocence but Toni's heart raced. This meant more frustration, more quarrelling. *Oh, Lord. That's all we need. Please let this pass without too much trouble.*

For a fleeting moment she thought she might keep this information from Blake. Let the puppy be killed and save herself and her fellow travelers the trouble that would surely come from knowing Mr. Kane killed the rooster and framed the dog.

She warmed some beans from last night's pot and made a fresh batch of biscuits. Ginger liked them warm with honey, and since Toni felt like she owed her friend after snapping at her earlier, she pulled out their stash and decided to be generous with the sweet treat.

As much as she tried to forget her conversation with

Alfred, Toni found it impossible. She honestly wasn't the same woman she'd been just three and a half short months ago. The old Toni wouldn't have a bit of conscience over saving the train some tension by sacrificing a dumb mutt. But when she scanned the train and found Alfred sitting crossed-legged in front of Wolf, while Mrs. Kane looked on, she knew she couldn't allow it.

As luck would have it, Mr. Kane sauntered off from the wagon train just as darkness fell. Toni grabbed her shawl. "I'll be back," she said to Ginger.

"Where are you going?"

"To the woods."

"I'll come with you."

"Ginger. No," she said. "I need privacy."

"Oh, for mercy's sake. I won't look. But you know the rules. No one goes off alone."

"Ginger, listen to me. Please respect my need for privacy."

The woman frowned and looked as though she was about to refuse. But as her eyes perused Toni's face, she nodded. "Everything all right, though?"

"It will be." Toni smiled. "Trust me. And thanks."

Stealthily, she followed Mr. Kane through the woods until they reached the river. He seemed to be waiting for someone, so Toni remained hidden. It didn't take long for the mystery to be solved. In a moment of revulsion, she realized that Mr. Kane was meeting a woman—someone that wasn't his wife. The two embraced and Toni thought she might be ill. Now wasn't the time to confront the horrid man and she certainly wasn't going to stay around to watch.

Behind her, the ground crackled, just as she turned on her heel to head back to the wagon. She gasped as she came face to face with Ginger. Her face was twisted in rage as she looked on toward the direction of Mr. Kane and the woman. "That slimy snake."

"Ginger!" she hissed. "You promised to stay away. What about respecting my privacy?"

She nodded. "I was going to, but then I got worried." Her simple honesty touched Toni's heart, making it impossible for her to hang onto her irritation.

"So now you know, I was following Mr. Kane."

"Did you know he was with some floozy?"

"No. And that's not why I was following him."

"Then why?"

"Let's go back to the wagon before he hears us out here."

"It's too late for that." Dread clawed Toni's gut at the sound of Mr. Kane's voice. She turned to face him, relieved that the woman had apparently fled. But Mr. Kane's face, twisted dangerously and his hand shot out to grab her forearm. "What in tarnation are you doin' prowling around out here spying on me?"

Toni fought back a scream of pain as he nearly squeezed the blood from her. "I wasn't spying on you, Mr. Kane," She said.

"You best turn her loose before I fill your gut full of lead, mister."

Staring down the barrel of a Colt, he seemed to get the message and dropped Toni's arm. Which was most likely a good choice. Toni had no reason to doubt that the girl would follow through on her threat.

Ginger's outraged voice split through the woods. "You dirty rotten snake. Fooling around with another woman behind your poor wife's back. Don't you think she's been through enough?"

"What she's been through?" The man's eyes glittered dangerously in the light of the moon and he stepped forward looming above Ginger's small frame. "Do you think my wife has been through more than I have? Didn't we lose the same children? Two before we came west and then our little girl. Seems like everyone thinks she's sadder than I am. So if I take comfort in a warm, young thing that understands what I'm goin' through, that's my own business. And you best keep your mouth shut if you know what's good for you."

Even face-to-face with the giant of a man, Ginger didn't back down one iota. She raised herself to her full height and squared her slim shoulders. "Don't you dare threaten me, mister. I don't scare very easy."

"You better, if you know what's good for you."

She stomped her foot like a petulant child. "I said don't you dare threaten me, you dirty warthog."

Toni figured now was as good a time as any to step into the middle of the fight. "Mr. Kane, I wasn't going to bring this up right now, but I'm afraid you've left me no choice."

"What are you talking about?"

Swallowing hard, she gathered a breath. "I know Wolf didn't kill the Adams' rooster."

His sneer was immediately replaced with something akin to fear. But he recovered just as quickly. "I ain't got no idea what you're gettin' at."

"You do too!"

"Ginger, please," Toni said. "Stay out of this."

"Well, he does."

This time she kept her tone a little more firm. "Let me handle it."

"So-rry!"

Good Lord, the girl was more trouble than she was worth at times.

"Mr. Kane, you were seen tossing the rooster to Wolfie. There's no denying that it was you."

"Try to prove it." He shoved past the two women and crashed through the woods back toward the wagon train.

Ginger nudged her. "Who saw him?"

She stepped forward, headed back toward the wagon train. "Alfred," she whispered.

A profanity escaped Ginger's lips. "Oh, well, that ain't gonna be no help, is it?"

"I don't know. Probably not."

"Why do you think Mr. Kane would frame his own dog?"

Toni shrugged. "I couldn't even begin to guess. And you should stop swearing."

"What for?" Ginger asked. "I like swearing."

"For mercy's sake." The girl was difficult. "You should stop because it's not Christian to swear. And besides, it doesn't sound very ladylike."

Ginger chortled and slung an arm around Toni's shoulders. "Toni, you know I ain't Christian nor a lady, so what difference does it make?"

"If you'd give God a chance he could heal whatever wounds you're trying to cover up. Look what he did for me."

Ginger dropped her arm. "Don't try to save me, Toni. Preachin' ain't gonna do no good. I got my mind made up about God and what I got to do no decent Christian could get away with as far as the Almighty's concerned."

The words terrified Toni. Ginger was her own worst enemy and the girl didn't even know it. Or if she did, she didn't care.

"All right, listen. What are we going to do about Kane?" Ginger said in a huff.

"I don't know yet." She cast a sideways glance at the young woman. "This entire situation is much bigger than I am. And I'm going to pray and ask God for wisdom; and according to the book of James, He will give it to me."

"I know what I'd do," Ginger said. "I'd walk right up to that fella, stick a gun in his belly and force him to tell the truth."

"I don't think that's going to work in this situation, Ginger. Please don't do anything of the sort."

Ginger let out a huff and stomped on ahead toward the wagons.

Toni followed. She recognized this awful position. She wasn't a gossip. Wasn't one to tell tales. She never had been, even before she became a Christian. But if she told anyone about Mr. Kane and his dalliance with the unknown woman, she could put herself in danger of being made out to be a liar. Who would believe a former prostitute over a respected member of the wagon train?

She began praying for wisdom before she even reached her wagon.

Charles Harrison watched his son as he played with the half-wolf puppy tied to the Kane's wagon. The boy was the spitting image of his mother—so much so that it was impossible for Charles to look at him most days without the pain robbing him of breath. His Cordelia had a bond with the boy that Charles had resented from time to time. As much as it shamed him to admit it, even to himself, he'd been jealous of the attention Delia showered on the child. They shared a love of animals, of nature. Of just about everything.

"Alfred," he called. The boy turned to him, a simple look of trust in his eyes.

"Hi, Pa."

"Time to tell Mrs. Kane and Wolfie goodnight and come to our campfire."

"Yes, Pa." He stood, patted Wolf on the head. The dog whined and licked Alfred's hand. The boy laughed. "Okay, Wolfie, see you tomorrow."

"Good night, Alfred," Mrs. Kane said. Her sad eyes never failed to touch Charles's heart. She'd suffered much, this woman. But then, so had most of the pioneers. Still, it seemed as though she might be just a little more fragile than others.

"Night, ma'am," Alfred replied.

Mr. Kane entered the campsite, anger exuding from his

body. Before Charles could move, the massive man snatched Alfred by the front of his shirt. "You been telling tales about me, boy?"

"Hi, M-Mr. Kane."

"Turn my boy loose," Charles said, fingering his pistol. Outraged, he wasn't sure what he'd do if Kane didn't do as he was told.

"Not 'til he tells me what he's been sayin'. I know it was you, you dimwitted fool."

"What happened?" Mrs. Kane asked.

"Never you mind. This boy knows and he best admit it before I beat him to death with my bare hands."

Rage shot through Charles at the threat. He slipped his Colt from his holster and shoved it toward the man. "I said get your hands off my son, or I'm going to plug you full of holes, Kane."

Mr. Kane turned. Charles kept his eyes firmly on the man, knowing Kane was sizing him up. After what seemed like forever, he turned Alfred loose. Charles stepped forward, keeping his Colt pointed squarely at the man's chest. "No one threatens my family, and if you ever lay your hand on him again, believe me, I won't give you a warning first, I'll just start shooting."

A sneer curled Kane's lip. "You keep that half-wit away from my wife and my dog. You understand me?"

"He won't come near your wagon again." Charles slipped his arm around Alfred's shoulders. "Come on, Son. Let's go."

"Okay, Pa. Night Mrs. Kane. Night Wolfie. Night Mr. Kane."

Mrs. Kane lifted her hand. "Goodnight Alfred."

Charles heard the sorrow in her voice and once again his heart went out to her.

"Go on," Kane growled. "Get out of here and don't come back."

Without another word, Charles led his son back to their own wagon. Belinda looked up when they walked to the fire. "Want some coffee, Pa?"

Charles looked at his daughter. At thirteen, she wasn't a little girl anymore. When had she changed so much? And why hadn't he noticed? Delia would be so disappointed in him if she could see him now.

Fifteen

Timothy wept when they arrived back at the site of the attack. He fell across his wife's grave. The sounds he uttered were more like that of a wounded animal than human. The sounds and sight were chilling.

Sam turned away to allow the man his privacy, but nothing could stop the sounds of Timothy's anguish. While Brian took a rifle and went in search of game for supper, Sam surveyed the area, looking for signs that might lead to a clue of some sort. One thing he knew for sure, someone had been in the camp since the travelers had left. He doubted Swooping Eagle and his men had returned. More likely, stray Indians or men headed for the gold fields passed by looking for anything salvageable. At least the graves hadn't been disturbed.

Finally, after searching in all directions from the burnt wagons and debris that had been left behind after the attack, Sam found enough footprints and broken branches to give the three men a starting point, at least.

At first light, they would cut north from their current position and track in that direction. With a little luck and a lot of help from God, he was hopeful the trail would remain clear.

As the three men sat around the campfire later, Brian remained pensive, Tim sorrowful. Sam prayed. He had never been one to press his religion on anyone. Or any of his feelings and beliefs. He had always felt a man should do what he thought was right. But Timothy's grieving was deeper than normal sorrow. It was soul-wounding pain that only Jesus could heal. And Sam knew he had that hope, himself. How could he keep it from a man who so desperately needed the same peace?

"I just don't understand how this could happen to her," the man said, weeping into his already soaked handkerchief. "She was the sweetest, gentlest woman in the world. She was good and kind and loved me and Janey. Why did God take her when we need her so?"

Anytime a man asked a question, Sam figured it was an opening to give the best answer he knew. And that answer could only be one thing.

"We live in a fallen world, Tim. Wars and killing are part of this sinful nature of man. Only Jesus is perfection and we won't know perfection until we live in the heaven designed for Him. Your Sophie was caught in the middle of man's sinful nature."

"How is it to be borne? I can't breathe. I can't sleep. All I can do is see her with that arrow through her heart, staring at me and begging me to do something to help her." Sobs racked his body, deep engulfing sobs that gripped Sam's heart. He went to the man and clasped him on the shoulder.

Timothy grabbed him and clung. Sam offered the man his strength. "How do I hold on?" Timothy cried. "How?"

Sam searched his heart and allowed the words to flow from a place inside of him where he knew God inhabited. "Maybe you don't have to be the one to hold on. Jesus will hold on to you until you can raise your arms again, Tim. His love will carry you and when you can carry your own weight again He'll still be there, walking right alongside you."

Timothy remained silent for the rest of the evening. Sam wasn't sure if he had helped or not, but he prayed throughout the night that God would give Tim the peace he needed to focus on the task at hand.

When dawn broke, the three men mounted up and turned their horses northward. Sam only prayed that they weren't in for more heartbreak if they did find the captives.

So far, so good. Toni remained cautious but hopeful as the wagon train moved out with no demand from Curtis and Lucille Adams that Wolf be killed for the loss of their rooster. She wasn't sure why the couple was being so quiet about it, but for now it was a mercy.

Her heart went out to Alfred, though. He didn't understand why he couldn't play with the dog and that just didn't seem fair to Toni. When Ginger offered to drive the wagon so she could walk for awhile, she accepted readily and walked with Fannie. It was the first chance she'd had to really share her frustration with her friend and it felt good to get it out.

"I just don't understand how Mr. Kane can be so cruel to a boy as sweet as Alfred."

"Maybe he's just trying to ease Alfred's pain when the dog is put down."

"What do you mean?"

Fannie looked back, her brow creased. "Toni, Wolf killed Curtis's rooster. That man has already been to Blake demanding the dog's death. Blake just doesn't have the heart to do it right now with members of the other wagon train just having lost so much. We have five new families with us and each has lost a family member. There's just too much death right now. He might give the dog one more day, maybe two, but Blake knows what has to happen."

Toni thought about the secret she carried and decided now was the time to share with her friend. She gathered a breath for support. "Fannie, I have to tell you something. I'm not sure how it will effect Blake's decision, but . . ." She told Fannie about Alfred's revelation and Mr. Kane's reaction to her accusation. She didn't leave anything out. Not even the woman who met Mr. Kane.

Coming from the background she did, not much shocked Fannie, or Toni either, for that matter. "You didn't see the woman's face?"

Toni shook her head. "It was already getting dark and they were a ways off. She ran when they heard us talking."

"If we could find out who the woman is, we might use it to force Mr. Kane to confess."

"But how do we do that without sneaking around ourselves and suspecting every woman in the train?"

Fannie snorted. "Well, don't look at me."

The very thought brought laughter to Toni's lips. "Trust me, the thought never entered my mind."

"Toni, look at Alfred."

Toni followed her gaze and compassion squeezed her heart. Alfred walked about six feet behind the Kane's wagon where Wolf was tied. He spoke to the animal, but following Mr. Kane's instructions stayed far enough away so that he couldn't be accused of disobedience.

"And they say he's a dimwit," Fannie said with a laugh. "Looks to me like he found a way to get around Mr. Kane's demand."

A smile played at the corners of Toni's lips. "Still, it's so sad."

"I'll talk to Blake. But he can be so dadburn stubborn, I can't promise he'll believe Alfred about Mr. Kane, and even if he does, he might not feel like he can interfere."

"I understand." Toni kept an eye on Alfred. When a horse rode up beside the boy, she frowned. "What's Kip doing?"

Fannie's brother rode alongside Alfred. He said something to the lad, reined in his horse and Alfred climbed up behind him. A wide grin split Alfred's round face and he waved like he was riding in a parade. "Would you look at that?" Toni said. "Who would have thought Kip could be so sweet?"

"No kidding," Fannie said. "I guess they both like animals. That's something they have in common."

"Well, at least riding behind Kip will give Alfred something else to think about for awhile."

"In the meantime, I'm going to do my best to make sure that pup isn't put down."

Charles watched his son climb onto the back of the massive horse behind Kip Caldwell. A twinge of worry struck him, but when he saw the grin on his boy's face, he couldn't help but smile and figure it would be all right. Alfred had precious little happiness these days. What would it hurt for him to ride a horse with a friend and enjoy himself for awhile?

Charles had so much regret. Regret that he had been so ashamed of that boy all of his life. Or maybe it was more disappointment in knowing he'd never be the son he had dreamed of. The sort of son who would work side by side with his father. Would plant their fields and bring in the harvest, and eventually marry and bring a bride to the land of his inheritance. All the grandiose things he'd imagined as a father . . . none of that would ever come to pass. The disappointment had been too much for Charles. Only now did he see his selfishness for what it was. And his family had suffered for it. Could he ever make up for his shortsightedness?

He held tightly to the reins as his oxen pulled hard against the rocks. When he looked up again, Mrs. Kane walked alongside his wagon staring up at him like something was on her mind. What on earth?

"Good day, ma'am."

Her gaze darted forward to the wagon where her husband drove their own team, and back. "Listen, I want to give Wolf to Alfred. Do you mind?"

"But I thought . . ."

"I know. I know he's supposed to be shot in a couple of days, but I think if he belongs to Alfred, no one's going to have the heart to do it."

Ah, so she had an ulterior motive. Charles's guard shot up. He gave a nonchalant shrug. "Maybe, maybe not." Since Alfred was a baby, he'd been the victim of cruelty and not just from other children. To his knowledge not one person had ever done the right thing just to spare the boy's feelings.

She gave him a wry grin. "Don't think it's because I'm being noble or thinking just of the boy. I can't bear the thought of losing that animal to a bullet. As much as I care about Alfred, he's a means to an end, right now."

A strange admiration flowed through Charles at her honesty. "I didn't figure you were being noble. Not too many folks are where my boy is concerned. But I like the idea of keeping that pup alive if we can."

"You know, Mr. Harrison. I didn't think you loved that boy. But I can see you do. I'm glad."

She smiled, warm like a spring day, and Charles's spirits lifted.

Sixteen

After a week of rain and wind, the Cheyennes' trail had gone cold and Sam was getting farther and farther away from the wagon train. He wasn't sure where to go next, despite the fact that the two farmers looked to him for guidance and assurance at every turn. They reminded him of a couple of children with no idea where to go next.

"There's an old trading post about six miles from here," he said pointing north and east. "I suppose we could give that a try. Trappers still come down from the mountains although there aren't very many left. The best I can suggest is that we make our way there and ask around. The Indians don't bother the trading posts too much because they do their own bargaining there. If Swooping Eagle and his warriors are still in the area, someone will likely have seen them."

Tim nodded. "Let's go, then." In his voice was a tension that bespoke an understanding that time was running out.

Everything within Sam wished he could offer hope, but he agreed with the man's unspoken assessment. Unless they could gain information at the trading post, there was little chance those captives were going to be found.

It took the better part of a day to travel the six miles. Even though the rain had, mercifully, ceased, the horses had trouble keeping sure footing in the sludge and the going was almost as slow as travel by wagon. Sam could feel Brian and Tim getting more and more frustrated with the pace.

Thankfully, the shack stood before them, weather beaten and not that sturdy-looking, but the smoke puffing out from the chimney was a mercy, as Sam hadn't been altogether positive the place still existed. They dismounted and tethered their horses to the hitching post in front of the building.

Inside, the odor was strong enough to knock a man flat on the dirt floor. Between the hides, tobacco smoke, and just plain sweat and leather, the place could use some fresh air.

The grizzled mountain man who owned the place looked them over when they entered. He sized them up without speaking. His dirty buckskins reeked and Sam fought to keep from pinching his nose to keep out the stench.

A quick scan of the room revealed a one-legged old-timer perched on a pickle barrel, whittling on a hunk of wood. In a corner sat an Indian woman, probably younger than Fannie if Sam had a guess. She glanced up, looked him over without apparent interest, and then went back to her sewing.

Sam inclined his head toward the man. "Afternoon."

The bushy-faced man gave his own nod. "What brings you men to these parts?"

Timothy started to step forward, but Sam held him back. If Swooping Eagle were a regular customer, the proprietor

wasn't about to give out information to three strangers without some profit.

"We're looking for a Cheyenne war chief. Swooping Eagle.
Heard of him?" Sam could see by the twitch of the man's eye
that he knew exactly who Sam was asking about. And if the
fear in his eyes was an indication, it wasn't going to be an easy
task to extract the information they desperately needed.

"I ain't in the business of looking to get myself scalped."

Sam forced a short laugh. "I understand." He glanced
around. "I could use a buck knife like that one."

"You can buy out the whole dadblamed store and it ain't
gonna do you no good."

Movement from the corner caught Sam's attention as
the Indian girl stood. Sam noted her protruding belly as she
walked to a back room.

The trader paid her no mind, but kept his gaze on the
three of them. "Still want that buck knife?"

Brian tensed, and Sam knew he couldn't keep the young
hothead back any longer. He didn't even bother to try. "Look,
mister. That redskin took my sister, and I aim to get her
back. You best start talkin'."

"Well, men. I'm truly sorry for your trouble, but I got
my own troubles to consider. Move on out and we can part
company friendly-like."

"Friendly?" Tim stood shoulder to shoulder with the other
man. Together they made an imposing image. "That savage
killed my wife and took my daughter, and I'll be hanged if
I'm leaving here before you give us the information we came
for."

The man gave them a squinty-eyed stare and before he moved a muscle, Sam knew what was coming. In a flash the trader whipped out a shotgun from beneath the counter and pointed it straight at Tim's chest. "I ain't tellin' you again. I don't sell information that's gonna get me kilt. Get on outta here. If you come back you won't leave alive."

Sam could see that both men were trying to weigh the possibility of overtaking the trader. They might have tried it, but the old-timer across the room pulled out a rifle of his own. "You fellas best do as my boy says. I ain't got as much patience as he does."

One gun was bad enough. Two would get all three of them killed before they could go for their own side arms. "Let's go, men," Sam said, clasping each man on the shoulder, he applied enough pressure to get their attention away from a fool's errand.

"Let's *go*."

Finally, the two men seemed to grasp the gravity of the situation. They backed slowly toward the door and made it outside without a bullet through the heart. Sam mounted his horse with a prayer of thanks and led the way down a steep, rocky path.

The three men remained silent for the better part of a half hour until Tim broke the silence, his voice trembling with anger. "Now what?"

Sam wasn't sure. But one thing he felt certain about was that the trader knew where the Cheyenne war chief was holed up. But there was no way he'd be talking any time soon. "Swooping Eagle is somewhere close."

"How do you figure?" Brian asked.

"The trader knows where he is, he wasn't surprised about the captives, which means he's likely heard the Indians talking about it, or possibly saw them for himself."

"Why, that weasely varmint. He saw my sister and didn't lift a finger to help her?" Brian's anger flashed in his eyes and shook his hands as he gripped the reins. "I've half a mind to . . ." He whipped around. In a flash, Sam moved his horse to intercept.

"Don't be foolish. If you go back, you'll be killed before you even get off your horse."

"What are we going to do, then?" The desperation in Tim's tone matched the same emotion playing across Brian's face. Sam's heart went out to the two men. Now wasn't the time to abandon them or suggest they give up. They would have to continue their search, even if their efforts proved futile.

Just as he was on the verge of suggesting they ride west, the sound of footfalls coming after them at a running pace met his ears. He placed his finger to his lips to silence the other men. Brian and Tim each drew their pistols. Sam held up his arm for them to wait just as the young Indian girl from the trading post came running into view, her face twisted in fear, chest heaving from the exertion. One hand rested on her belly. She ran forward and grabbed his horse's bridle and spoke in perfect English.

"Take me with you. I beg of you."

"Get on back to your man, Squaw," Tim growled.

Sam held up a silencing hand to the man. "Wait, Timothy. Let the woman speak."

Dismounting, Sam removed his canteen from his saddle and offered it to her. Gratitude settled over her features and she reached for the canteen, drank deeply and handed it back to Sam. She wiped her mouth with the back of her hand. "If you take me with you, I will show you the camp of Swooping Eagle."

"She's lying." Tim's hatred infected the very air.

Brian leaned forward. "Have you seen the captives?"

Her braids bounced as she nodded. "Two days ago. Cheyenne war party stopped at the trading post. They traded for whiskey and guns."

Alarm filled Sam. "What did they trade?"

"Horses and pelts." She averted her gaze, raising Sam's concern.

"Is that all?"

"Two children."

"Was there a little red-headed girl?" Tim asked, panic swelling his tone.

"Swooping Eagle did not part with that child. She is to be a gift to his sister who lost a daughter last winter to illness."

"Over my dead body!" Timothy growled. That's my little Janey." He jumped from his saddle and grabbed onto the woman's arm before Sam could intervene. "Tell me where that Cheyenne camp is, or I'll do worse to your face than that man of yours ever did."

Sam was about to step in, but Brian beat him to it. "Let her go," he said. "It ain't her fault what that evil trader done."

"What will he do with the children?"

Her face clouded. "When the Pawnee come to trade, he will sell them for protection."

Sam heaved a sigh. "The children would be slaves."

She nodded. "If they were taken by Cheyenne or Sioux, they would become part of the tribe. But not so with the Pawnee."

"When will the Pawnee come to trade?"

"They come each new moon."

Three days. Not much time. "How many days to reach the Cheyenne camp?"

"You will take me with you?"

"Tell us!" Tim growled stepping forward menacingly again. Sam intercepted him.

"If you threaten this woman once more, I will not allow you to ride with us any farther."

Tim fell into angry silence and retreated to his horse.

Relief covered the young woman's features. "My name is Yellow Bird. I am Dakota Sioux. My father was deceived by Orlan, the trader. He promised to care for me. But he has only been cruel. H-he says he will trade my child to the Pawnee when it arrives. I must not stay with him any longer. Will you allow me to accompany you?"

"Why not simply return to your people?" Brian asked.

Her face clouded. "I cannot return in disgrace. My father is a great chief. My presence would shame him."

Sam's heart went out to her and he made a swift decision. "You may come with us."

"She better know where that camp is," Tim muttered.

"You have my word." Her quiet response seemed to soften

the man a little. He swallowed hard and inclined his head briefly.

"You may ride with me." Sam climbed into his saddle and reached down for her.

"Miss," Brian asked, inching his horse alongside Sam's pony. "Did you see a grown woman with the Indians? M-my sister was the only woman taken."

Yellow Bird nodded. "She was with the Cheyenne."

"Was she . . ." He cleared his throat. "H-how did she . . . ?"

Yellow Bird pressed her hand on the man's arm. "Your sister was treated well. She was not violated."

Brian's face crumpled and Sam thought he might fall from his horse, so great was his relief. "Oh, God. Thank you, thank you."

"However, you must retrieve her quickly. She is a lovely young woman and will become the wife of a warrior soon. If you do not reach her first, it will be too late to trade for her."

Instantly, Brian's demeanor changed and he steeled his features. "Then let's go."

Toni couldn't help but keep her gaze focused on the horizon, searching for Sam's return. As the days went by, she became more and more convinced that given a little encouragement, he might come to realize that she could be a good wife, no matter her past. Then the guilt always followed. He had his convictions, didn't he? What kind of a woman would knowingly try to cause a man to go against the thing he truly felt was right?

Even when she came to grips with the fact that she would never belong to him, she felt his absence so great it hurt. His was an irreplaceable presence.

Grant Kelley had taken Sam's place as the head scout for the time being. Which, of course, angered Ginger, who felt she was the better tracker.

"It's because I'm a woman," she pouted over a warm supper of rabbit stew.

"Blake says Grant's more experienced."

She held her fork midway to her mouth and glared. "And you believe hogwash?"

Toni knew better than to say yes, so she took the coward's way out and shrugged. "I'm not an authority on tracking."

"Well, I am. And believe me, that Grant Kelley is as green as a newborn babe. And I don't care who hears me say it."

Toni could well imagine the young woman was telling the truth about not caring who heard her say anything. She'd proven herself to be a hothead and a big mouth, and most of the folks in the wagon train steered clear of her.

Truth be told, according to Fannie, the only reason Ginger was allowed to stay on the tracking team was because Grant intervened for her sake. Blake was all set to banish her to water detail after the last time she failed to recognize the signs of three deer before she spooked the animals and the wagon train was forced to forego fresh meat for the fifth night in a row. She'd definitely not been very popular, until she defied strict orders from Blake that no one was to leave the camp alone and went after the animals, tracked them down, and brought home a doe and a buck, thus redeeming herself in the eyes of all. Even Blake, who growled at her for disobeying his orders, accepted Grant's request to keep the girl riding scout.

Toni had to wonder why Grant always seemed to take Ginger's side. He watched her closely, but not necessarily with the eyes of a man who was smitten. As a matter of fact, most of the time his brow was creased with a bewildered frown. Toni had always considered herself a fair judge of a man's intention, but Grant Kelley confused her. She wasn't sure where his thoughts led when he looked at Ginger.

The girl was vehemently against the very notion of Grant as a suitor, though Toni had no idea why. Personally, she thought the girl could use a strong man like Grant. But it was none of her business and definitely not worth risking Ginger's ire. So she'd stop bringing it up.

Ginger wiped her mouth with the back of her hand and gulped down the last of her coffee. "That was right good, Toni."

"I'm glad you liked it." The summer evening was a little warm for a fire, and many had decided to forego a personal campfire in favor of cold leftovers from the night before, but Toni knew Ginger couldn't abide cold food that was supposed to be warm or warm food that should be cold, so she'd decided to put up with the heat.

"Wouldn't it be nice to get a breeze?" Toni asked.

"Blake says we should reach the South Pass in a week or so and nights will be downright cold."

"Good. At least if it's cold we can cozy up to the fire or

cover with a blanket. When it's hot, there's nothing to do but sweat."

"We could go swimming," Ginger suggested. Then her eyes brightened. She leaned forward and lowered her voice. "Toni, let's do go swimming."

"We're not allowed."

"Hogwash. Why do those men always think they can tell us what to do?" She dipped her plate in the dishwater, scrubbed a little and used a dry towel to wipe it. "I'm going swimming. You coming?"

"Of course not." Toni frowned at her companion. "And you can't either. You'll get into trouble."

"Blake Tanner ain't my pa." She gave a belligerent scowl. "What's he gonna do? Take me to the woodshed for a whippin'?"

Toni's lips twitched, and despite her better judgment, she couldn't help but imagine the soft waters of the creek just a few yards away. "We'll get caught."

"Shoot. No one's caught me yet." Ginger grinned and leaned in close. "We'll walk a mile up the creek. We'll be back before anyone even knows we're gone."

Only a moment's hesitation stopped Toni. Then a hot breeze blew across her, fanning the summer flame and sending a flash of heat down her spine. "Okay, count me in."

Ginger slapped at her thigh. "That's more like it! We'll leave in another hour after things settle down around camp. I'm goin' off to check on the animals."

A grin played at Toni's lips as she watched the girl stomp away from the campsite to make sure everyone's animals were accounted for. She set about cleaning up supper dishes. Once finished with that chore, she grabbed a fresh cup of coffee and settled onto the tongue of her wagon and waited for Ginger.

She was just beginning to wonder if her friend was coming back, when Amanda Kane wandered into their camp. "I'm not bothering you am I?"

"Of course not." Toni stood and grabbed a clean cup. "Have some coffee?"

Amanda fanned her face with her flat hand. "Goodness no. It's much too hot."

"I suppose." Toni settled back onto the tongue of the wagon and invited her newfound friend to join her.

"Thank you." She pulled her skirts aside and sat.

"What brings you by tonight?" Toni asked. She had to wonder if Amanda knew her husband was dallying with another woman. But she figured they weren't close enough friends for her to bring it up. Although she still kept her eyes open, hoping to find the identity of the woman in question, she wasn't going to be the one to bring up the infidelity to Amanda.

"Oh, nothing in particular, I suppose. My evenings are pretty lonely since Becca went away."

"I'm sorry. I can imagine your grief."

The woman's eyes filled with tears so quickly that Toni was caught off guard. "Do you know what's worse?"

Shaking her head, Toni reached out and took Amanda's hand. The woman clung to her, almost painfully. "My husband is a scoundrel."

Toni swallowed hard. "What do you mean?"

"He's breaking our marriage vows." Amanda's tears stopped and an angry spark replaced the sadness. "With an-other woman."

"Are you sure?"

"A wife knows." She thumped her chest. "He can't fool me. And I don't think he's even trying to. It's almost as though he wants me to find out."

"For what purpose, Amanda?"

A shrug lifted boney shoulders that had gotten even bonier since her daughter's death. "I'm not sure. He should know I won't dishonor God or my family with a divorce." She shuddered. "Can you imagine the outcast I'd become in polite society?"

The question struck Toni as funny and she gave a short laugh. "I can well imagine."

Amanda's eyes grew wide and she gave a gasp. "Oh, for mercy's sake. I'm sorry, Toni. I didn't even think."

Ginger chose that moment to stumble into camp. She glanced at Amanda with poorly concealed impatience. Amanda seemed to pick up on the fact that she was no longer welcome. She stood. "I suppose I'll turn in."

Toni placed a hand on her arm and frowned at Ginger. Honestly, the girl's rudeness needed to be addressed. "We're going swimming," she said, keeping her tone low.

Ginger groaned. "Why don't you just tell the whole wagon train!"

"Hush, Ginger. Amanda's not going to say anything."

"Of course not." The woman's face split into a grin. "Especially if you invite me along."

Toni smiled and nodded. "I was just about to do that."

"Oh, for heaven's sake." Ginger gave a huff. "Just be sure you don't go blabbing to no one else."

Amanda smiled at Ginger, obviously not a bit offended by her surly attitude. "You have my word."

"Let's go, then."

Seventeen

Sam could have kicked himself for being so easily detected by the Cheyenne sentries. Even under the cover of darkness, they hadn't gotten within five miles of the village without being spotted and captured. Now the three men and Yellow Bird were being escorted into the village, surrounded by what seemed like the entire tribe. They'd been divested of their weapons but otherwise allowed to remain untethered and on their own horses. That courtesy gave Sam reason to hope they'd come out of this with their hair intact.

Nearly naked children followed them in the torchlight and curious women as well. But no one accosted them. Much to Sam's relief. Perhaps the Indians didn't look upon them as enemies. Hopefully Brian and Tim would be able to keep their heads. The guards halted them and ordered the captives to dismount in front of a painted tipi. Sam knew this was the dwelling of a chief. And he had an idea exactly which chief they were about to face.

He felt Tim bristle when Swooping Eagle exited the dwelling. The war chief was even more impressive up close than he'd been from a distance. Sam couldn't help but admire the way he held himself. Shoulders erect, face like stone. Sam's eyes wandered to his arm. Toni had been right. The Indian had a healing wound much like the one on Sam's chest.

He stared back at Sam and his eye twitched slightly with the knowledge of what had caught Sam's attention. "You have come to trade?"

"You have captured one woman and four children." Sam pointed to Brian. "The woman is this man's sister."

Tim spoke for himself. "Give me back my baby girl." The threat in his tone was unmistakable and the warriors nearby tensed, poised to step in.

"Pa!" The scream pierced the air. Tim whipped around.

The little red-headed girl broke free from her captor, an Indian woman wearing a beaded dress made of deer hide.

"Janey!" Timothy ran toward his daughter, only to be grabbed by two burly warriors. They threw him roughly to the ground. He thrashed and fought until they had the better of him. One warrior held a knife to his throat.

"Pa! Don't hurt him, please. Ple-e-ase don't hurt my pa."

The Indian woman gently took Janey. She spoke softly in her Indian tongue. The child obviously didn't understand a word, nor did she stop fighting the woman. "Let me go. I want my pa!"

Swooping Eagle glared down at Tim. "You have no regard for Cheyenne village?"

"Chief Swooping Eagle," Sam said, keeping his tone calm

and quiet. "This man is grieving the loss of his woman. And now his child. He meant no disrespect."

The Indian stared hard at Tim, then spoke a sharp command in his native tongue. The warriors around Tim put away their knives and jerked the man to his feet.

Janey's cries could still be heard from somewhere inside a tipi, and Sam knew it took all of Tim's control to keep from once more attempting to run through the crowd and find his daughter. Thankfully, reason seemed to outweigh his impulse. He kept his gaze forward and stood perfectly still between the two warriors who had been ordered to stand guard. Which was a good thing, because Sam knew if he tried anything else, nothing Sam said or did would make a difference. Tim wouldn't live through the night.

Swooping Eagle studied Sam, his glittering eyes scanning his face. "You are not white?"

"My father was white. My mother was Sioux."

"You choose the white man's world?" He spoke with contempt.

"My mother left her people before I grew to manhood. I did not choose the white man's world. It was not my decision."

"Come. We will discuss trade." The Indian turned and entered the tipi.

"What about us?" Brian said.

Sam rested his hand on the young man's arm. "You're too emotional. Stay here and try to keep Tim calm."

"You give them whatever they want for my sister. You hear?"

Sam didn't respond. He had a sinking feeling this elaborate capture was designed for one reason: the war chief's desire for the woman Sam loved.

Toni and Amanda followed Ginger down the river until they reached a spot far enough from the camp where they wouldn't be heard or seen. The walk had heated them even further so none of the women hesitated to undress down to their bare skin. Side by side, they waded into the cool, refreshing water.

"Now ain't you glad I suggested a swim?" Humble, as usual, Ginger dipped under water and splashed back up, spitting water from her mouth.

"I sure am," Amanda said with a giggle. "I can't remember the last time I took a night swim. Come to think of it, I don't believe I ever have swam beneath a moon." She took in a deep, long breath and stretched her back staring at the night sky.

Ginger gave a grunt. "Well, that ain't much of one, is it?"

Toni floated on her back as well, and stared at the sliver of moon. "It'll be new moon in a couple of days, won't it?"

"Yes," Amanda replied. "I always prefer the beginning of the moon cycle. I like beginnings."

"I like the light of the full moon," Ginger said. "This one ain't even worth looking at."

"I'm just glad to get cool," Toni said. It was a night to relax and talk nonsense. She suspected Amanda must feel the same way.

Ginger tensed and stared toward the bank.

"What is it, Ginger?" Toni asked.

"Shh."

"Is someone there?" Amanda's voice trembled.

"I said Shh!"

"S-sorry."

A branch crackled. This time Toni heard it. Fear shot through her belly. *Please don't let it be Swooping Eagle.*

Squinting toward shore, Ginger stood perfectly still as the source of the noise came into view. She gasped. "A bear."

"What?" Toni hissed.

"A bear." Ginger repeated. "He must have smelled our clothes."

Irritation shot through Toni. "Your clothes, you mean. I hope you see now that you have to bathe regularly."

"This ain't no time for lectures. Stop acting like you're my ma, anyways."

"W-would you two stop arguing before he decides to come in after us?"

The bear rummaged about on the bank. "What's it doing?" Amanda hissed.

"What do you think, you numbskull?" Ginger whispered back. "Looking for a meal that supposed to be in the clothes."

A few minutes passed and it turned as though it would walk away.

Toni started to breathe easier. "Thank heavens," she whispered, just as the beast dropped to the ground and rolled onto its back.

Amanda moaned a little. "Merciful heavens. It's not going to leave. D-do you think it's waiting for us?"

"How'm I supposed to know?"

"Can you never be pleasant?" Amanda's tone rang with irritation. "I vow your surly attitude doesn't win you any friends."

"Who says I want friends?" Ginger shot back. "Besides Toni, here."

"Why don't the two of you save this argument for another time?"

Amanda gave a sigh and shivered. "Oh, never mind. If we make it back to camp alive, I say we let it go."

"That's fine by me," Ginger said.

The bear rolled onto its side and let out a long happy groan.

"Looks like we're in for a long night."

"Y-you don't think there are any snakes in here, do you?" Amanda asked.

Ginger swung about to face her. "What do you think?"

"Oh-oh my." Raw fear spoke in her voice, and then panic. "I hate snakes. I have to get out of here."

"Would you rather be eaten by a bear?"

"Why can't we get out on the other side?"

"That critter has our clothes," Ginger said, and Toni was beginning to wonder if the girl was indeed incapable of being kind to Amanda. "You want to walk naked into camp?"

Toni chose the water, the snakes, even the bear to walking naked anywhere. "I'm not going anywhere without my clothes."

Ginger's head bobbed in agreement. "Same here."

Two hours later, they were no closer to leaving the river

than they had been the minute the bear arrived. Their skin wrinkled, their bodies grew cold, and they shivered as the water temperature dropped. And still the bear kept vigil. As though waiting for the women to give up and become a willing meal.

"I'm starting to think that varmint's going to wait us out," Ginger said, her voice a mix of anger and fear.

Amanda's teeth chattered. "We have to get out of the water or we'll catch our deaths of cold."

Ginger gave a snort, "If we get out of the water we'll be dead, anyway."

"Shh," Toni said. "I hear someone talking out there."

"You sure?" Ginger frowned. "I don't hear nothin'."

Amanda cocked her head to the side. "I do, too" she whispered. "Someone is out there."

"For mercy's sake," Ginger exploded. "Which one of us is the scout, here? If there was someone out there, don't you think I'd be the one to . . ."

"Bear!!" a man's voice bellowed as a woman's scream sliced through the summer air.

The panicked cry from the shore put a stop to Ginger's outrage. "Get in the water, you idiots!" she called.

Without waiting for a second invitation, two shadowy figures splashed into the river. The bear stood on the shore staring into the water. Toni held her breath, her mind conjuring the image of the enormous animal deciding to come in after them.

It reared up on hind legs and let out a fearsome growl, then as quickly as the animal had appeared, turned and loped off. The relief in the water was palpable. All three women turned to the new additions to their adventure.

"Is that you Mr. Kane?"

"How is it you are out here with my husband?" Amanda's icy voice addressed the woman who stood shivering in Mr. Kane's arms.

Shock zipped through Toni as she realized just who that woman was. "Lucille Adams?"

Ginger let out a moan. "Lord have mercy."

Just as Sam suspected, the war chief was only interested in one trade. Toni for the rest of the captives still in his camp.

"We do not trade one person for another," Sam said. "Miss Rodden has made it clear she does not wish to be your woman."

A sneer twisted the war chief's lips. "You would allow a woman to cause war between us?"

"Would you?"

The Indian sized him up, then sat quietly for a moment. Sam respected the silence. He knew Swooping Eagle had more on his mind, otherwise Sam would have been dismissed.

He only had to wait a couple of minutes before Swooping Eagle spoke. "My mother was a great medicine woman."

Sam remained still while the warrior came to the point.

"When I was just a boy, the great Eagle granted her a vision concerning me. This vision foretold my many victories in battle."

The chief spoke with a hint of pride. Sam knew the best thing to do was to feed the Indian's ego. "Swooping Eagle is a great war chief. No one disputes that fact. You are respected among the white man." Respected might be a bit of a stretch, but the soldiers definitely took notice when Swooping Eagle wreaked havoc with wagon trains headed west.

Patience was wearing thin and Sam figured the Cheyenne war chief's days on the warpath were numbered before the soldiers came after him. They would not let him get away with it for much longer.

"My mother's vision also foretold the day when the white man would try to take our lands. They would invade by wagon. Kill the buffalo, push the Cheyenne from their lands. I alone would lead my people and other tribes of the plains against these whites."

The Indian spoke with such conviction, his words brought a chill to Sam's soul. Swooping Eagle had enough victories in battle to be a formidable foe on a small scale. If other tribes rallied behind the Cheyenne and joined them on the war-path, the loss of lives—to Indian and settlers alike—would be devastating.

"The white man doesn't want war," Sam said, but his words fell flat into the air. And rightfully so. He scarcely believed them himself. "The land is vast enough to make room for all people, Indian and white alike."

"The white man is not interested in sharing the land. He takes what does not belong to him and then destroys whatever he touches." He thumped his brown, bare chest. "But I will drive the white man from our land. We will lance them like the boils they are and drain their disease from our forests." He turned to Sam, his glittering black eyes boring into

Sam's. "The white woman is the medicine for which I have waited."

"Toni?"

"My mother's vision foretold of a white woman with hair the color of the snow. This woman would give me the strong medicine I require to triumph over the white man. The spirits have sent her to me."

Alarm seized Sam. Desire was one thing. Lust, he could have negotiated around, but if Swooping Eagle truly believed Toni was the medicine he needed to drive the white man from his land, he would stop at nothing to possess her.

There was nothing more to say. Sam only prayed that the Indian chose to let them leave his camp in peace. They'd have to find another way to rescue the other captives.

Eighteen

"Please don't let on about this. I'll be an outcast." Lucille's sobs echoed off the trees as they walked back to camp. It was all Toni could do to keep from turning around and giving her a stinging slap. The foolish woman had ruined two marriages and all she could do was cry because she'd been caught.

"If you don't tell your man, I will," Ginger said. "You deserve whatever you get as far as I'm concerned." She jerked her thumb toward Amanda. "You've wronged the nicest woman in this whole outfit, except for Toni here, and you did it for a worthless varmint of a man. That just proves you ain't got no brains." She stepped so close to Lucille, Toni thought she was going to shove her full bodied. Instead she stared at her, nose to nose. "Get out of here before I knock you on the ground." Still sobbing, Lucille ran toward the wagon she shared with her husband.

Mr. Kane hadn't even tried to take up for his mistress while Ginger raked her over the coals. And his cowardice disgusted Toni even more. He remained insolent and unrepentant.

Amanda, the woman wronged, refused to speak until they reached Toni's wagon. Then she turned to Toni. "May I stay with you?"

"You mean for tonight?"

"For good," she said with a determined lift of her head. "I'm leaving this man."

"You sure can!" Ginger said for them both. "Oh, well. If it's okay with Toni. You ain't gonna make this woman go back to Kane's wagon, are you?"

Toni truly hated to become involved in a situation between husband and wife, but under the circumstances, how could she turn the poor woman away?

"You ain't stayin' with any ol' whore, Mandy." Mr. Kane grabbed her by the wrist. "Now you be reasonable and come on back where you belong."

Ginger stepped forward, and glared at Mr. Kane. "She belongs wherever she decides she wants to be. So you best turn her loose. And what have you been told about calling Toni a whore?"

"Mind yer own business. You oughtta be takin' care of a man of your own instead of tryin' to be one." He dropped Amanda's wrist and stood over Ginger, his face twisted in such rage that Toni's heart raced as real fear knotted her stomach.

Ginger stood her ground. "I ain't scared of you."

"What's going on, here?"

Grant Kelley's voice spoke through the darkness a second

before he stepped out of the shadow and into the light of the campfire.

"Nothing you need to concern yourself with," Ginger shot back.

"I'll decide what I concern myself with and what I don't." Grant eyed Mr. Kane. "Is there a problem, Kane?"

Amanda spoke, her voice tight, strained. "Toni and Ginger have graciously agreed to allow me to share their wagon and Mr. Kane isn't happy about it."

"You place is with me, woman. And I ain't havin' you make a fool out of me."

"Kane!"

Toni joined the others, swinging around at the sound of a man's bellow. Curtis Adams stood before Mr. Kane, a bloody knife in his hand. His body shook from his head to his feet. "You and my wife . . ."

"Now, don't do somethin' stupid," Mr. Kane said, eyeing the knife.

Horror filled Toni as she, too, stared at the knife. "Mr. Adams," Toni said softly. "Where is Lucille?"

"In hell. Where she belongs."

Ginger expelled harsh breath and muttered an oath. "I best go get Blake."

"Wait, Ginger." Grant held up a restraining hand. "I don't know what's going on here. But from the looks of it, there's already been one murder." Grant already had his pistol drawn and pointed at Curtis Adams. "Curtis, you don't want to add another to your name, do you?"

"A man's got a right to avenge his family." Curtis spoke

through trembling lips and clenched teeth. His breath drew and released in spasms that shook his chest and shoulders. "My Lucille would never have betrayed me if this man hadn't somehow convinced her to do it."

Mr. Kane, idiot that he was, gave a snort, clearly baiting the distraught husband. "That's what you think. She flashed those big blue eyes at me the first time I seen her." He scanned the rest of the group, carefully avoiding his wife's gaze. "It weren't never my fault. That wife of his seduced me, if you want to know the truth of it."

A guttural growl rose from Curtis, and he moved faster than anyone could stop him. Amanda's scream pierced the air as Curtis hit his mark and the two men fell to the ground. Curtis jumped to his feet and ran away. Toni looked down in horror at Mr. Kane. The knife protruded from his chest and he lay lifeless where he'd fallen.

The entire wagon trail reeled from the news of betrayal, adultery, and murder in the very heart of the wagon train. This was one time Blake wished like the dickens that Sam was around to offer his wisdom and godly counsel in the midst of all the confusion. But in Sam's absence, folks looked to him for spiritual leadership. Reluctantly, he stood over three graves, spoke words of grace, and hoped to heaven the three of them stood before Jesus and not the other place. But who was he to know if they'd repented before death claimed them? The two caught in adultery and the man who had ended their lives. Three lives destroyed and one woman shattered.

Curtis had run away before Grant could catch him and

the gunshot that occurred seconds later told the story of his suicide.

As several men shoved dirt into the graves, the somber group sang "Amazing Grace." There weren't many mourners. Very few members of the wagon train were in attendance. After all, how could two adulterers and one murderer deserve a Christian burial?

Blake didn't necessarily agree with the assessment. And he performed his duty as he would have no matter who had died.

Noticeably absent was Amanda Kane. The poor woman had finally had enough. She'd buried three children and declared she would not pretend to be sorry this man who had made her life a misery was dead. Blake had declared that the Adams' wagon and goods would be sold among the travelers and all proceeds would go to Amanda. But she'd flat-out refused. She didn't want anything from the Adamses or from her late husband. Not very logical, but Blake figured a woman had a right to be a fool if she chose to be.

Beside him, Fannie sniffed and pressed her handkerchief to her nose. "It's such a waste, Blake," she had said hours before. "All those lives devastated because of sin. Senseless sin. Why would Lucille and Mr. Kane stoop so low when they had perfectly good marriages of their own?"

Blake had no idea. He'd never seen a model for marriage that worked for him. And until a couple of months ago, he'd been dead set against the entire institution. The fact that he'd ever married Fannie in the first place still made him dizzy. He was a blessed man, but bewildered nonetheless.

He slipped his arm around his wife and held her close. His heart soared as her head rested against his shoulder communicating her love, trust, and confidence in his ability to steady her. The two remained thus as the other folks in attendance began to leave the gravesite. In light of the events of the last twenty-four hours, Blake had called a halt for the rest of today. Tomorrow the band of travelers would come to the mouth of the Sweetwater River and Independence Rock. That should lift their weary spirits.

Amanda worried Toni more than she could say. The woman stared at that diary over and over. What had Blake been thinking, giving her Lucille's diary? What could that woman possibly have to say that would interest the woman she had wronged? But Amanda had decided to take it. "Maybe I'll be able to make sense of what they did if I read it in her own words." And so she'd taken it. The two of them had been riding side by side all day and Amanda had yet to say a word. It was as though all ability to speak had left the woman. Even when Toni spoke to her, she didn't reply. Just stared at the pages as though unable to look away.

She was actually relieved when Ginger rode up on Tulip. "Want a break?" she asked. "I'll drive the wagon if you want to walk."

"That would be nice. Thank you."

Ginger looked at Amanda. "How 'bout you. Want to stretch your legs a mite?"

Amanda's silence didn't sit well with the forceful woman. "Amanda! Snap out of it."

"Don't bother," Toni said with a sigh. "She's been like this all day."

"Well, that ain't right." Before Toni could react, Ginger snatched the diary from Amanda's hand. As though shaken from a state, the woman snapped her head up with an indignant frown. "What do you think you're doing?"

"Reminding you how to have manners." Ginger tucked the diary inside her jacket pocket. "I'll give this back later, after you take some time to walk with Toni."

Confusion clouded her eyes. "You want me to walk?"

"Oh, for heaven's sake," Ginger snapped. "Get out of the wagon and follow Toni." She led her horse to the back of the wagon.

"It's all right, Amanda," Toni soothed, holding her hand out to the woman. "Let me help you down." Forcing a gaiety she was far from feeling, she smiled. "I don't know about you, but my body feels like a big bruise. I vow, the last ruts we came through were about two feet deep. It's a wonder we ever got through them without breaking a wheel."

Ginger returned from tying Tulip to the back of the wagon.

"You two enjoy your walk."

Toni nodded. "Thanks for the break, Ginger."

"No problem. Grant came back from scouting and said we'll be at Independence Rock in a couple of hours. You just walk however long you want."

Amanda took a deep breath. "This is welcome. I didn't realize my legs had gotten so stiff."

She hadn't realized her own name over the last few hours.

But Toni refrained from mentioning the fact. Instead, she slipped her arm around her new friend. "It's easy to lose track of time." Truth be told, the woman had seemed to be in a daze, but now she seemed to be coming out of it, as though waking up from a light sleep. Very odd. Toni had seen it before but couldn't quite put her finger on where.

Amanda turned her head and stared across the horizon, a faraway look in her eye. "Zach killed the chicken and fed it to Wolfie."

"Lucille wrote that in her diary?"

Amanda nodded. "They wanted Wolfie dead so that I would go crazy. Lucille was with child and believed the baby was Zach's."

Nausea curdled Toni's stomach. "Wh-what?" Surely she'd misunderstood.

"Apparently, Zach convinced Lucille that the only way they could be together and raise their child was if I was gone for good." She shook her head, her eyes filling. "I almost went crazy when Katie died. Zach was convinced losing the next thing I loved would complete my insanity."

"Oh, Amanda. That's just about one of the most evil things I've ever heard."

"I suppose love can make a man do evil things."

A bitter laugh flew from Toni's throat. "Trust me, what that husband of yours felt for Lucille Adams had nothing to do with his heart."

"Then why would he do such a horrible thing to me just to be with her? Just because he knew I'd never give him a divorce?"

Toni gave a helpless shrug. "Sam says that sometimes the harshness of the trail and the sorrow of loss will do crazy things to a man or a woman. Zach's mind must have been half gone with grief."

"I wonder why he didn't just murder poor Wolfie instead of trying to turn the whole wagon train against the poor puppy."

"Because cowards never do their own dirty work," Toni said bluntly.

"He figured with my mind gone, he could drop me off at the nearest asylum and forget I ever existed."

Amanda's lips trembled.

"He didn't have any idea how strong you truly are, Amanda."

"Oh, Toni. I'm the weakest of women. After Katie died in that twister, I truly felt myself slipping away, over and over. You know, the funny thing is that Lucille Adams came to our wagon every day to sit with me, bring meals. Her friendship brought me back from that dark place. Until Wolfie started killing off their chickens. But I guess by then she already had her cap set for my husband. So the scheme took shape between them to make me go away."

"That's just evil and wicked and . . . and . . . despicable."

"Yes. But he's the one who's dead. And his lover." An odd smile settled across her pale lips. "But Wolfie is still alive and I'm sane. So I suppose there is justice in this world after all."

Her words sent a chill down Toni's spine. Looking into

the woman's half-closed eyes, she wasn't at all convinced of Amanda's sanity.

Sam's heart burned with regret that he'd ever told the two men the terms of getting the captives back. Neither came out and said it, but he could see their minds spinning with possibility. He'd made it clear there would be no trade and that the soldiers would have to be brought in to make the rescue. For now, they'd made a decision to at least rescue the two little girls still at the trading post. Yellow Bird had told them exactly where the girls were hidden in the back room.

Grateful for cloud cover, Sam fingered his Colt as he crept toward the back door. He lifted the leather latch to open the door. He winced at the loud creak. Stopping in his tracks, he held his breath until he heard loud snores coming from the other room. The trader and the old timer, he hoped.

Without making a sound, he entered the storeroom where Yellow Bird had instructed him the girls were being kept. Two pairs of wide eyes greeted him as he pulled aside the curtain and entered the filthy room.

He put his finger to his lips and motioned for them to follow him. They stared, unmoving as though frozen to the floor. He knew they weren't bound. Yellow Bird had told him as much. The trader had other ways of forcing submission. And that bruise across the cheek of one of the girls was proof of that. Anger spilled over him at the sight, but he kept his voice steady so as not to alarm the children. "I'm here to rescue you," he whispered. "But you must stand on your own and walk out. I cannot carry both of you."

One by one they got the message and stood.

"Good," he whispered. "Follow me."

They obeyed, silently shuffling along the wooden floor. Sam's heart raced as he stood aside and nudged each child out the door ahead of him.

"What the . . ."

"Run, girls!" he called. They took off without being told twice. Sam saw a shimmer of a gun barrel and dove out the door as rifle fire shattered the air.

Nineteen

Sam's head pounded and he had trouble focusing on the terrain before him. According to Tim, he must have hit his head on a rock as he dove out the door of the trading post the night before. Brian had been right there covering him while Tim crawled forward and pulled Sam to safety. Sam felt like a darned fool for allowing himself to be wounded that way. It had taken a couple of greenhorns to save him.

Pride certainly did go before a fall, he supposed. He was proof of that.

The trader fired off a few shots, but gave up pretty quickly. Yellow Bird confided he wouldn't come after any of them. He was simply too lazy. That much was good news.

Yellow Bird still rode behind him. For which Sam was grateful. If not for her rigid strength, he'd most likely have fallen off his horse hours ago. The child she carried moved around as though anxious to be born. Sam had never experienced such a feeling in his life.

Yellow Bird apologized the first time the baby kicked against his back, but Sam quickly assured her he didn't mind. A miracle in the midst of chaos and heartache was never a reason to apologize.

The afternoon sun was just beginning to disappear behind a western ridge of mountain along the horizon when the wagon train came into view.

Sam urged his horse forward. It didn't take much to convince the beast that he would finally be allowed to rest.

Tim galloped ahead of Sam and broke off his momentum. "Hold up, Sam. We gotta talk." Sam had been expecting some sort of negotiation, but he'd hoped to wait until he'd had the opportunity to speak with Blake. Certainly not now when his head spun with each movement of his horse. But his injuries didn't seem to dissuade the two men in any way. "The way Brian and me see it, we saved your neck back there at the trading post. You owe us."

"What did you fellas have in mind?"

"You know what I'm talking about," Tim said.

Brian took up the other man's cause. "We're taking that woman to Swooping Eagle. It ain't like she's gonna be missed by anyone. She ain't got family, and that Indian ain't gonna hurt her. Besides, we both know what she was before. Who else would marry her?"

Outraged, Sam fought against the nausea.

"We do not trade one human being for another," he said.

"It ain't for one other," Brian insisted. "It's for my sister and Tim's little girl plus little Bridie Long. That's three lives for one whore with no one who cares if she lives or dies. How can you be so derned stubborn?"

Anger welled up white and hot, making his head spin even more from such strong emotion. But he was in no shape to force anything at the moment. "We will not speak of this again," Sam said firmly.

He nudged his mount forward as shouts from the camp indicated they'd been spotted. He had to remember to ask Blake for extra guards around Toni. There was no telling what these desperate men might do.

The force of the wind on top of Independence Rock whipped Toni's Lindsey-wooley skirt about her legs and stole her breath from her lungs as it gusted into her face.

"I can't believe I let myself get roped into climbing this confounded rock. It ain't nothing more than an upside-down bowl of granite. Wish I'd just gone for a dip in the Sweet-water River instead."

Ginger's complaining was beginning to grate on Toni's nerves and she was starting to wonder why she'd even bothered to coax the young woman to come along. Sometimes Fannie had noted that there wasn't a lot to like about the girl, but Toni felt a strong loyalty to her. It was hard not to care about someone who only saw the best in you.

And, despite what anyone else saw, the fact was that Ginger had a good heart. Much better than she wanted to let on. But mainly, Toni had been afraid she'd defy Blake's orders and go swim in the river after all.

Ironic, really. At one time they could barely get the girl to scrub the dirt from her body. Now she was the first one to water whenever they camped alongside a place suitable for swimming or bathing.

"I'm finished," Amanda announced, the last of the four women to use the paint.

"Then let's go."

"Do you three want to go bathe when we get back? Blake says we're headed out first thing in the morning."

That sounded good to Toni. Plus she wanted to change into her clean dress and scrub this one. "Let's."

"Blake won't mind as long as we're all together. But one of us will have to stand guard while the others bathe. Then we can switch."

Only Amanda hadn't said anything. They turned to her. She shook her head. "I don't think so. I have . . . something . . . else I planned to do."

Ginger frowned. "Like what?"

Amanda hedged. "I-just . . . it's . . ."

Toni decided to spare the woman the necessity of sharing something she obviously wanted to keep to herself. "It's perfectly fine if you want to stay in camp, Amanda."

"I just thought we were supposed to take baths so we don't stink."

Amanda laughed. "I promise I'll wash up so that I don't start offending."

Toni and Fannie joined her in the laugh, and slowly Ginger's ice cracked and her face broke into a wide grin. "All right. You probably don't need a bath as bad as the rest of us anyways."

They were about to start the descent down the rock—a descent that Toni feared would be much more difficult than the climb up—when shouting from the camp below caught their attention.

"Hey, look over there!" Ginger's voice rang with excitement as she pointed over the wagon train to the horizon beyond. "Unless I miss my guess, Sam's back and he brought them prisoners with him. Let's get going. I want to hear all about it."

Toni's heart skipped several beats and her mouth suddenly went dry. So much had happened since Sam had been gone. Things that he would have helped her get through had he been there.

Even now, at the sight of him, she longed to sit with him and allow his gentle voice and godly wisdom to help her make sense of the deaths of three men and Amanda's heartbreak over the entire situation, although thus far she hadn't even so much as shed one tear for her murdered husband. Not that Toni knew of, anyway. She had allowed Ginger to give Lucille's diary to Blake, and Wolfie was officially exonerated for the crime of rooster killing, although there was no one left to insist upon his punishment anyway.

Amanda had decided to allow the pup to remain with Alfred. A gesture that relieved Toni. It wasn't that she didn't like the dog. But with Ginger, Amanda, and herself sharing the cramped wagon, there wasn't much room for an animal that was growing larger by the day and was starting to look more and more like a wolf.

The dog's bark signaled that he too saw the returning wagon train members. Toni's face felt flushed, but she didn't care. She couldn't wait to see Sam. A nudge to her ribs brought her attention around to Fannie. "Are you going to climb down and go see him, or make him wait?"

A smile curved Toni's lips. "I'm going."

Blake frowned with concern at the size of the knot on Sam's head. He could see that his friend was in no shape to be reporting on the rescue just now, so he ordered him to his bedroll without allowing two words to escape his lips. "Get some rest," he ordered. "There'll be plenty of time to talk about this a little later."

"Wait, Blake. I must say one thing first. The rest will wait."

"All right. One thing." Blake relented. "What is it?"

"Keep Toni protected."

"Don't worry, my friend. I've been keeping an eye on her. Besides, she's now sharing her wagon with two other women." His lips quirked into a grin. "And one of them's Ginger. She can shoot straight as most any man."

"No. Listen. She needs extra guards. Swooping Eagle is determined to have her."

Blake sensed there was more to his friend's concern than simple overprotective instincts for the woman he loved. He looked around for the two men traveling with Sam. His eyes scanned the camp but they were nowhere to be seen.

Several of the women in camp had descended upon the rescued children and they were being cared for. The Indian woman who had arrived with Sam remained at his side. Blake looked down at her belly. Just what they needed, one more pregnant woman to join the twenty others that were in various stages of pregnancy. "Ma'am?"

The woman looked up, her brown eyes filled with question, but she didn't speak. "Can you tell me what happened out there?"

Her eyes held a hesitance that only worried Blake more. "Please. Sam's in no shape to fill me in and the two men who were with you are gone."

She gathered in a long breath and nodded. "I will speak of it with you."

"Thank you. Please sit down. My wife went to the rock, or she'd be here to get you something to drink. I can offer you some water."

She nodded. Blake ladled a dipper full of water into a tin cup and handed it to the young woman.

She thanked him, took a sip, then met his gaze head-on. "The Cheyenne chief will make a trade. A white woman he desires for the woman and two children still in his camp. He has vowed that if you do not agree, there will be more battles and he will not stop until the woman is his. He will wait only two weeks."

Blake's heart sped up. So that was what prompted Sam to

make him promise to add guards. "Were you a captive of the Cheyenne as well?"

She took another sip and shook her head. "The trader, Orlan, took me from my father's village. I have been living with this man as his woman for many moons. Two-Feathers helped me to escape."

Blake nodded. "Swooping Eagle allowed the other children to leave?"

She shook her head. "He traded them to Orlan. Two-Feathers rescued them as well."

The light in her eyes when she spoke of Sam indicated her admiration for his friend. Blake approved. If Sam was determined not to marry Toni because she was a white woman and he half Indian, then perhaps he would turn his eyes in the direction of the pretty young Indian woman. If Sam fell in love with an Indian girl, maybe he wouldn't feel like he had to be alone forever.

"This child you are carrying," he said pointing toward her stomach. "Orlan is the father?"

"Yes."

"Will he come after you?"

She shook her head. "He would have traded my child to the Pawnees, and perhaps me with it. He had grown tired of me and planned to bring a new woman into the trading post before winter."

"I take it you'd like to stay with the train? Or do you wish to go to your people?"

"I will stay," she said quietly. "If you will allow it."

Well, he couldn't very well turn a woman out in her

condition, could he? He'd just have to figure out what Sam wanted to do about her and let his friend handle the situation. He had more important issues to consider. For instance, protecting the wagon train against an imminent attack from the relentless war chief.

Twenty

Misery poured through every bone in Toni's body. She felt like she was on the verge of a screaming, hissy fit. Every time she observed Sam walking with the beautiful Indian girl, or accepting food from her hands, her throat closed up and all she wanted to do was yell, cry, throw a big rock, and get Sam's attention. He'd barely spoken two words to her in the week since they'd left Independence Rock, despite the fact that he'd insisted upon adding guards to her wagon.

Now they were headed through South Pass, and during a time when she should be starting to get excited about passing from the eastern part of the country into the western, she could only think about Sam and wish that Indian girl had stayed with the trader. Though it made her feel guilty to think such a thing. Still. . .

Walking next to Fannie, she felt a little better, but not much. "Listen," her friend said. "You have to stop worrying about Sam and Yellow Bird. There is nothing between them."

Toni gave a snort and nodded toward the young Indian girl who was stirring a pot over Sam's campfire. She looked awfully comfortable. "Are you sure she knows?"

Fannie followed her gaze. "Well, maybe she doesn't, but Sam isn't one little bit interested in her."

"Any man is flattered by such obvious attention from a woman. Believe me, I know."

"Blake says that's just her way of showing her gratitude because Sam rescued her from that trader."

"You mean acting like a wife? Cooking for him? She even takes care of his horse, for mercy's sake. His horse! He saved me too, but I don't clean up after his animal. Maybe that's the problem. Perhaps if I do those things he'd notice I'm still alive."

Fannie gave a short laugh.

Toni turned on her, scowling. "What's so funny?"

"You. You're jealous, aren't you?"

"Don't be ridiculous. Of course I'm not jealous." Toni drew in a sharp, cool breath. "Do you think I am?"

"I'd bet on it."

"No wonder love can drive a person crazy." Toni pressed her palm to her stomach. "I suppose I must love him."

Fannie's jaw dropped. "Are you telling me you didn't know that already? Truly?"

"I suppose not. What do I know about love?"

"Oh, Toni. Toni. Love is wonderful."

Affection rose in Toni for her friend. She knew Fannie truly meant what she said, but the truth of the matter was this: Love was only wonderful when the person you loved returned your affection. Sam would never belong to her. And staring at him now, as Yellow Bird stood over a campfire stirring a pot of something that was surely supper for Sam, it was clear to see the two made an equally lovely couple. A woman about to give birth, a man waiting for his meal. What could be more fitting for Sam?

Sam knew Toni deserved an explanation. Especially after the way he'd kissed her the night before he left. But somehow it was too difficult to explain that he owed something to Yellow Bird as well. After all, he'd taken her from her home—granted she had begged him to do so, but they were the only two Indians on the wagon train and he felt a responsibility to watch over her. Plus, she would need help once the child was delivered. And that would happen very soon.

That didn't mean he cared for her in the way he cared for Toni. Nor could he ever. Still, the fact remained Yellow Bird seemed like a good match for him. And he was willing to be a father for her child if that's what God was asking of him. He couldn't just turn his back until he knew for certain.

Others in the wagon train had noticed it. Women who never gave him a second glance before Yellow Bird's arrival now sent him amused grins and knowing glances. He supposed it wouldn't matter who the Indian woman might be. As long as she was Indian, folks assumed her to be a suitable match for the only man around with Indian blood flowing through his veins. Did they even know or care that they weren't of the same tribe? Did it really matter?

Probably not. Red skin was red skin. His bitterness surprised him, though. Anger, really. Resentment that the one woman he loved more than life itself was off limits to him, but the one everyone found suitable didn't make his heart sing the way Toni did.

Yellow Bird handed him a bowl of good-smelling buffalo stew and corn cakes to sop it up with. Guilt bit through him even as his mouth watered from the delicious aroma. Here she was heavy with child and serving him. He reached out and took her wrist. "Sit down next to me and have some."

She shook her head and backed away. "I will eat after you have had your fill."

It was clear that even though she'd lived with a white man and clearly knew a white man's ways, Yellow Bird insisted on behaving as though that part of her life had never existed. "That isn't the way of things here, Yellow Bird."

"It is the way of our people." Her quiet admonishment sent irritation scrambling through him.

"I'm half white too." Why couldn't anyone seem to remember that? It wasn't that he discounted his Sioux heritage. But neither did he discount his white blood. "Sit down and eat your supper with me or I will dump mine out and go hungry."

"I will eat as well, Two-Feathers." Yellow Bird dipped a ladle full of stew into a tin bowl and sat on the ground next to the campfire.

Wolfie's bark captured Sam's attention and he turned toward the sound. Charles Harrison and his two children were having dinner with Toni, Amanda, and Ginger. Jealousy nearly ripped a hole in Sam's heart at the sight of Toni smiling at Charles as he pulled off a hunk of meat and tossed it to the ornery dog.

No wonder the animal stole food and refused to learn obedience if his owner insisted upon allowing such poor manners. Wolfie gobbled up his treat and begged for more. Toni's laughter carried on the wind, clutching at Sam with a longing to be the recipient of that smile and gaiety. But no, some widower was edging him out. He scowled.

"You . . . care for the white woman. Yes?"

He jerked his head back to Yellow Bird, ready to deny her observation. But the solemn look in her dark eyes told him plainly there was no point in denials. "Yes."

"Then you will marry her?"

He gave a short laugh. "Not hardly."

"I do not understand."

"A white woman does not marry an Indian in the white world."

She cocked her head to the side, confusion still clouding her eyes. "You will not marry the woman you love?"

Had she not heard a word of what he just spoke?

"I can't."

A shrug lifted slender shoulders. "Then perhaps she would be better off joining Swooping Eagle's tribe."

The very thought sent knives of fear through his entire body. "Yellow Bird. Toni does not want to go with Swooping Eagle."

"Even if it means she could free the two hostages who have family here, and another child? She will not even consider this?"

Sam didn't know if she'd consider it or not, but there would be no discussion about that scenario while he had breath in his body. Besides, Toni had no idea that Swooping Eagle had even made the offer. Only five people knew . . . Sam, Blake, Timothy, Brian, and Yellow Bird. Sam had threatened Tim and Brian should they reveal the bargain to her, and of course Blake wouldn't breathe a word of it. Not even to his own wife.

Yellow Bird gave a jerky incline of her head. "You have not spoken of this with the one you call To-ni."

Sam made no apologies. "I have not. Nor will I."

"But perhaps she will choose to accept Swooping Eagle's offer. A Sioux woman has the right to refuse. Why should this woman not be given the same choice that your own mother was given to choose your father?"

"She has already refused him once." Granted, there were no other captives involved at the time, but Sam couldn't imagine Toni agreeing to such a bargain anyway. Nor would he allow her to do so.

Yellow Bird remained silent after that. She stood, her food untouched, and began to clean up. Despite her cumbersome burden, she moved with the same grace he remembered his own mother possessing. His long desire was to return to the Sioux nation and bring the gospel to his mother's people. Now that Yellow Bird had entered his life, he was beginning to question God. Was she the helpmeet he'd been waiting for? If so, he had no choice but to put thoughts of Toni from his mind and concentrate on getting to know the Indian woman.

She turned to find him staring. Her lips turned upward in a tentative smile.

Jerking to his feet, Sam handed her the empty bowl. "Thank you, Yellow Bird. The meal was tasty."

He turned his footsteps toward Miss Sadie's wagon. If anyone had the answers he was looking for, it would be the widow.

The creek rippled along a rocky bed as Brian and Tim stood side by side under the light of a half moon. The wind coming down from the Rockies caused a chill in the air, but Tim didn't feel a thing. The only thought he could concentrate on was that Indian woman with her dirty hands on his little girl while she screamed for her pa.

"We both know what we gotta do," he said.

"I don't know." Brian's tone was hesitant, which infuriated Tim. Now wasn't the time to get soft on the subject and change their minds.

"You want your sister to become a whore for some Cheyenne buck?"

Tim didn't even see the blow coming until he was on the ground staring up at the enraged young farmer.

"Don't ever talk about my sister that way again, you hear me?"

"Now you listen to me, Brian. I don't mean to be disrespectful of her. It ain't her fault she was taken by them savages any more than it was my Janey's fault. But you got to be realistic." At the risk of another punch hitting its mark, Tim continued, despite the warning in Brian's eyes. "That sister of yours is a right handsome woman. If we don't get her back soon, some Indian man is going to see the same thing and want her for his squaw."

"All right. You got a point. But don't ever call her a whore again. Is that clear?"

"I was out of line with that," Tim said, feigning contrition. "Now, let's figure out how we're gonna get this done."

Amanda had remained silent through most of the meal, her few smiles reserved for Alfred or Wolf. As much as Toni hated to admit it, the woman seemed to be descending into a darkness that Toni couldn't pull her out of. Despicable as he'd been, Mr. Kane had obviously known how fragile his wife had become. Toni had no doubt that losing that puppy back then might have sent her into insanity. As it was, the betrayal found in the pages of Lucille Adams's diary seemed to be more than poor Amanda could reconcile in her mind. The look in her eyes seemed almost vacant at times, as though she couldn't quite comprehend the sights, sounds, and smells going on about her.

Toni tried to draw her out as much as possible, but the past few days had been challenging. She barely spoke, barely ate. Toni felt helpless. Useless.

Father, what good am I to anyone if I can't even help my friend through this pain?

Toni slipped her hands into the dishwater and began scrubbing. Behind her Amanda moved and Toni turned to find her friend on her feet, heading away from the wagon. "Amanda, wait," she called. "Where are you going?"

"To the creek."

"You can't go alone."

"I'm not. I'm meeting Ginger."

Irritated, but relieved that she wouldn't be alone, Toni nodded. "All right. But it's chilly tonight. I wouldn't try to swim."

Amanda waved her away, leaving Toni feeling sheepishly like a mother hen. But truly, they could catch their deaths of cold if they tried to swim in the chilly waters this time of night.

Though it was barely August, the higher the travelers climbed in elevation, the cooler the nights were becoming. Just this morning, they had awakened to find frost on the ground. And the snow-capped peaks were all around them on the horizon. So despite the rugged terrain and craggy slopes, at least there was less heat to contend with.

Toni finished the dishes in just a few minutes and sat on the wagon tongue to enjoy a cup of coffee before retiring for the evening. As she replayed Amanda's words and actions in her mind she became more suspicious. At the precise moment she planned to go after her friend, Ginger walked into their camp.

"Where's Amanda?" Toni asked.

"Ain't she here?" Ginger poured a cup of coffee. "I can't be looking out for her all the time."

"Where have you been?"

"Playing poker with a couple of the hands."

The hands were unmarried men headed out west to work on ranches. And Ginger liked to sit around with them spinning tales and playing cards. Toni had warned her against getting a bad reputation, but the young woman didn't seem to care what folks thought about her.

"Where's Amanda?"

"That's the second time you asked me that." Ginger gave a huff. "How'm I supposed to know where she's at?"

Knots formed in Toni's gut. She snatched her shawl from the wagon and yanked Ginger along with her. "We have to go find her."

"Yow! Don't pull my arm off." She stopped short. "Wait a minute. You tellin' me Amanda's missing?"

"I'm not sure. All I know is that she said she was meeting you and the two of you were going to the creek."

"Do you know how dadblamed cold it is in that water?" she asked with incredulity. "Why would I be that dumb?"

Toni shrugged. "She caught me off guard while I was working on the dishes. Said the two of you were going."

"You think she lied to you?"

Now she was starting to understand. "It would appear so."

"Well, I best go find her before she wanders into the creek and gets herself drowned."

"I'm coming with you."

"No, you ain't. You can just stay right here where you won't get kidnapped by that Indian."

Toni couldn't help a little laugh. "Oh, Ginger, for mercy's sake. You know Swooping Eagle isn't anywhere near this place."

"I don't know anything of the kind, and neither do you."

That much was true. Still, Toni had to believe that since the Indians hadn't returned after all this time, that had to be a good sign of something. At any rate, she fervently prayed so.

"You stay here and wait for me," Ginger said again. "I'll go find Amanda."

But Toni was firm. "If she felt the need to lie to me in order to go off alone, there must be something wrong with her."

"You just figuring that out?"

Toni hated the coldness in Ginger's tone. "No. But I'd hoped she'd start to pull out of it instead of going deeper."

"Well, let's go, if you're determined to come along."

They found her at the creek.

"Toni, are you seein' what I'm seein'?"

Bewilderment washed over Toni and she couldn't seem to move. Amanda's clothes were on the ground. She stood naked in the moonlight, her arms in the air as she spun around and around.

"What in tarnation does she think she's doing?"

"Obviously she doesn't know what she's doing." Heartsick, Toni shook her head and fought back tears. "Oh, Ginger, she must be going mad."

"Maybe we oughtta go get her before she hurts herself," Ginger said. "I knew a man once lost his mind grievin' over his dead wife and son when cholera got 'em. He ran off into the river and drowned hisself just like that."

"Let's go." Toni moved with caution. "Be careful not to startle her. We don't know what she might do if we come up on her too quickly."

Moving with care, they reached the woman. "Amanda," Toni called softly. "It's Ginger and Toni. We're here to help you."

Amanda burst into tears at the sight of them. She fell into Toni's arms. "Help me."

Toni's heart twisted with compassion at the slurred cry for help. She stroked the woman's hair and prayed.

"Come on," she finally said, "let's get you out of this cold air." Amanda didn't even fight when the two women grabbed her clothes, helped her dress, and led her back to camp where they put her to bed. They slipped back outside the wagon and sat together on the ground against a wagon wheel.

"Should we tell anyone?" Ginger asked.

Bewildered by the whole thing, Toni shook her head. "I don't know." If Amanda came to her senses soon, she would be humiliated. But if there was any chance she might be a danger to herself or anyone else, didn't they have a responsibility to let others know?

Twenty-One

Blake cursed the day he'd decided to take one more wagon train of pioneers to Oregon. He should have left it at the last one like he'd intended and then he wouldn't be having all of these troubles. In the privacy of their tent, he said as much to his wife.

"You wouldn't have me either," Fannie reminded him dryly. She lay in his arms outside of the wagon that Kip and Katie shared. Her hair tickled his cheek, but he didn't mind. As a matter of fact, he sort of liked the feeling.

"You're the only thing good about my life these days," he grumped.

"Poor Amanda." Fannie's voice rang with compassion. "What can we do for her?"

"I've half a mind to leave her at Fort Bridger when we get there."

Fannie sat up, her red curls cascading down her shoulder and landing on Blake's chest. "You can't be serious."

"I said I've half a mind." He grinned and pulled her back

to his shoulder where she belonged. "The other half remembers that my wife would never speak to me again if I did it."

"You best listen to that half. Because it's right." Fannie fell silent but her breathing never shallowed, so he knew she wasn't asleep.

"Anything else on your mind?"

"No." She took a sharp breath, and Blake held his tongue knowing she was about to speak again. "Well, more of what we're already discussing, really."

"What do you mean?"

"I didn't think much of this until now, but Katie told me earlier that Amanda has been calling her Becca for a couple of days."

Blake frowned into the darkness. "What do you reckon that means?"

"I'm not sure, but if she's losing her mind, she might be imagining that Katie is Becca. On the other hand, she might just be thinking a lot about her daughter these days, and since Katie and Becca were so close maybe she's just misspeaking by accident."

"Could be. Never can be too careful, though."

"You're right. I think I might want to keep a closer eye on my younger sister."

Blake expelled a breath. "I'll set up a pallet for her on the other side of the tent. You go ahead and get her."

Fannie sat up again and stared down at him. "Thank you, Blake. We'll have all the privacy you want as soon as we get to Oregon and you build me that fine cabin you're always talking about."

"The one with our bedroom at one end and the twins' at the other?"

Laughter bubbled to her slender throat. "If that's what it'll take to keep you happy, then build the rooms wherever you want." She lowered her head and kissed him. When she would have drawn back, Blake held her firm and kissed her more deeply. He pulled back and reached up, shoving her springy curls behind her delicate ears. "I love you, Mrs. Tanner."

Her smile said it all, but still she whispered in the darkness, "And I love you."

Charles Harrison watched from a distance as poor Mrs. Kane struggled to pull herself together enough to stir the pot of beans she was watching for supper. He wished he had the gumption to ask if she could use his help, but women were so sensitive about their abilities in the kitchen, he didn't want to offend.

She stumbled toward the pot and would have rocked into the fire if she hadn't caught herself just in time to jerk herself upright. The close call was enough for Charles. He strode forward, then stopped as Amanda pulled something from her apron pocket and tipped it to her lips.

Was the woman drinking? If so, that would explain her bizarre behavior of late. He'd noticed the staring, silence, and absences from camp. He understood, or thought he did, the way grief could change a person. After all, he'd left his two children to fend for themselves for the most part after his wife's death. He'd been surly and unkind in his grief.

But that hadn't lasted long. And truth be told, Mrs. Kane's sweet acceptance of Alfred made a large contribution to his return to himself. If there was anything he could do for her, he wanted to repay her kindness.

He frowned as she, once again, tipped what looked to be a bottle, to her mouth. As he neared the campsite, the acrid smell of smoke stung his nose. He glanced at the pot of beans Amanda stood over but they seemed fine. With a frown, he glanced around, searching for the source of the burning. In an instant, his heart nearly stopped beating as a flame engulfed the bottom of Amanda's skirt.

Scrambling to action, Charles barreled against her, knocking her to the ground and covering her with his own body. He barely felt the burning as the fire slowly faded away. Folks hurried over until a crowd had gathered.

"What happened?" Sam asked. He was closely followed by the little Indian woman. She went to Amanda immediately and stooped down next to her.

"Her skirt caught fire," Charles explained.

Sam frowned and pointed to Charles's stomach. "What happened there?"

Charles looked down and saw the blood and the shard of glass protruding from him. He glanced at Amanda, but she remained oblivious. He shrugged. "I don't know."

"Well, you best go see Grant Kelley. He's the one who seems to know how to fix everyone up."

Charles hesitated. "It doesn't seem to be that bad. I could probably . . ."

"Don't worry, Mr. Harrison," Toni said. "We'll take care

of Amanda. You go on and have Grant take a look at your wound." Her eyes pleaded with him and Charles realized he wasn't the only one noticing Mrs. Kane's odd behavior.

"All right, Miss Toni," he said. "I'll be back later to see how she's getting on."

"Perhaps you should wait until in the morning. She has been exhausted lately and I fear she'll be asleep very soon."

Although he knew he wouldn't sleep a wink for worrying about the woman, Charles knew he had no choice. "Morning, then."

"Come for breakfast and bring the children."

He appreciated her gesture and would have smiled, but the pain was beginning to intensify in his stomach. He placed his hand over the wound and it came away with more blood than he'd realized. "I-I better go find Mr. Kelley."

"Wait a minute. That's a lot worse than it first appeared to be." Sam grabbed his arm. "I'll get you to your wagon." He turned to Kip. "Go get Grant."

"Yes, Sir." The lad took off, lickety split.

Pain sliced through Charles's abdomen as he opened his eyes and winced. Grant Kelley sat next to his pallet. "You got me all fixed up?"

"As long as you're still for a couple of days, you should be good as new. I had to stitch you up." Grant looked at him intently. "You want to tell me how part of a glass bottle got in your belly?"

Charles shook his head. He had his suspicions but wasn't

about to voice them aloud. "I can't tell you any more than you can tell me, I'm afraid. I stood up and there it was."

"After you put out the fire on Mrs. Kane's dress."

"That's right." Charles gave an uneven breath. "There must have been a bottle on the ground."

"That would be unusual, especially in Toni's campsite, don't you think?"

Charles frowned. "Look, I told you all I know. Are you accusing me of something?"

Grant gave him a frank stare. "Have you anything to confess?"

"What for instance?"

"I don't know. But unless I miss my guess, the part of a bottle I found in you came from laudanum. You know anything about that?"

Charles shook his head. "Laudanum? Not whiskey?"

"Whiskey?" Grant shook his head. "Different shape and size. You sure there's nothing you want to tell me?"

"You sure you're not accusing me of anything?"

A grin tipped Grant's lips. "I'm sure. It's pretty obvious you didn't know what sort of bottle ended up in your gut."

"No, I saw her drinking something just before her skirt caught fire, but I thought it was whiskey." Charles frowned again. "She's an awfully good woman. Been through too much in too short of a time. I wouldn't want to see her looked down on because of this."

Grant patted the man on the shoulder. "Neither would I. I'll do my best to keep it quiet. But I'll have to tell Blake what's going on. Addiction to laudanum is pretty severe. We just have to hope she's not been taking it long and she shouldn't have too much trouble."

"Anything I can do to help?"

"You rest and stay in bed until I tell you otherwise. Then maybe you'll be useful when she really needs someone to be a friend."

"When's that?"

"When she has to start remembering that her children and her husband are dead. Without the laudanum to dull her senses, she'll need all the friends she can get."

Charles watched him leave. His thoughts came to rest on the pretty widow. He'd hoped perhaps, when they reached Oregon, she might consider a marriage for convenience sake. He needed a wife and the children needed a woman's touch. But how could he even consider making a proposal to a woman in such desperate need of help? Or perhaps God had sent him for just that purpose. To help her heal.

Toni barely slept. Why did that Indian girl have to be so handy with bear grease to slather on Amanda's burns? Where had she gotten it anyway? She'd only been traveling with them for a little over a week. As much as Toni had insisted she could take care of Amanda, the Indian girl had insisted just as much that she would be the one to care for the burns.

Who did she think she was?

Even now, when the stench of the grease nearly drove Toni from the wagon, she wasn't about to go and leave this Yellow Bird creature alone with her friend.

Ginger stuck her head through the flap at daybreak and had five words to say. "Lord have mercy, that stinks."

"It will soothe her burns and keep the poison away," Yellow Bird spoke up before Toni could scowl and order Ginger from the wagon. The young Indian woman had the patience of Job and the wisdom of Solomon. No wonder Sam Two-Feathers had completely forgotten that Toni existed. In the light of this woman, Toni definitely walked in a shadow.

Jealousy so strong it hurt gripped her. "I'm leaving for awhile," she announced.

"Yes," Yellow Bird said softly. "You must rest."

"What about you?" Ginger asked. "I'll watch over Amanda while you get yourself some shut-eye."

Yellow Bird's face clouded with confusion. "Shut-eye?"

"Sleep. You know, you shut your eyes?"

Her sensual lips curved into a smile. "Yes, I know. Shut-eye. I will have some and you will watch A-man-da."

Ginger's face split into a grin. "You catch on fast. Blake says the men are going out hunting. They found a herd of buffalo a few miles south and figure we ought to get some food stored up."

"Two-Feathers is going to hunt buffalo as well?"

Toni stiffened at the woman's use of Sam's Indian name. It just seemed too familiar. As though the two of them had a special connection shared with no one else. Well, of course they did with them both being Indians, but unless Toni missed her guess, Yellow Bird wanted much more than camaraderie brought about by blood. She was looking to get married and Sam was the man she had in her sights.

"Nah," Ginger was saying. "Blake claimed rights to get in on this hunt. He's missed the last two. So it's Sam's turn to watch over the wagon train." She chuckled. "He ain't too happy about it neither."

The relief in Yellow Bird's face sent another wave of unease through Toni. This woman was staking her claim.

Ginger pointed to Yellow Bird's stomach. "When's that little papoose going to be born anyway?"

"Ginger!" Toni said, aghast.

But the Indian woman only smiled. Apparently Ginger had enchanted her somehow and the feeling was mutual. "It is all right. My baby is growing impatient. It will not be long."

"You think that trader's gonna come after you?"

Oh, for mercy's sake. The woman had not even a little sense of propriety. But again Yellow Bird didn't seem to take offense.

"The trader Orlan is not a good man. He will trade the baby to the Pawnee and also me if we go back, but no, I do not believe he will come after me. He tired of me after the baby began growing in me."

Ginger gave a bitter snort. "Just like a man. Get a woman with child and then lose interest when she gets fat with it."

Toni groaned.

Yellow Bird frowned as though trying to make sense of the words. Then they sank in and she giggled. Toni hadn't known Indian women even laughed in merriment. "I did not mind his loss of interest."

"I just bet." Ginger laughed and the two seemed to share

a moment that did not include Toni. Was this woman going to steal everyone that mattered?

Sam swallowed hard under Toni's scrutinizing gaze. Why had she come to the Bible study if all she was going to do was glare? Her arms were folded in telltale fashion and he could practically see her seething. It wasn't easy to share about the love of God while she sat there breathing fire that definitely was not divine. Still, he had a responsibility to follow through on the scripture he'd felt the urge to share.

"*God commendeth his love toward us in that while we were yet sinners Christ died for us*. Unconditional love means we make the right choice even before we see results or gratitude. The way Christ died on the chance that one person would accept his salvation. It's a dying to self and our own wants and dreams. Especially when giving up those dreams brings us pain. Jesus struggled against the cross. We see that when he prayed in the garden the night before he died. He asked his father to let the cup of death pass from him. But it wasn't possible and he ultimately allowed his love to compel him to the cross. Love doesn't always feel good. But it always leads us toward the right course for our lives."

Sam scanned the small group of travelers that had gathered for the Bible study. He dared to allow his gaze to fall on Toni. Pity clenched his heart, and when she looked back all traces of anger melted away by the salty tears flowing down her cheeks.

Twenty-Two

Toni awoke to the sound of Amanda's sobs. According to Grant, her burns should be healing well. But the sobbing grew worse. She seemed more alert, but unable or unwilling to carry on a conversation.

"Do you think the doctor has some laudanum?" was all she'd managed to say in a couple of days. Apparently she was in too much pain.

Toni's request to Grant Kelley had been met with a scowl. "Her burns aren't that bad. I've had worse shoeing my horse."

Amanda had cried when Toni relayed the message. And now she was crying again.

"Amanda?" Toni's voice whispered into the dark wagon. "Are you all right?"

"It hurts so bad. Toni, I have to have laudanum."

If she was in that much pain, Grant would just have to give her something to make her feel better. And if he wouldn't listen to reason, she'd go to Blake and force the issue. This refusal was nothing less than cruelty to a woman who had already been through unimaginable pain over the last few months.

"I'll be back as soon as I can," she said.

Amanda nodded. "Hurry, please."

Toni slid on her shoes, a worn pair of false button-up shoes with a low heel. She'd bought them from an officer's wife at Fort Laramie after her laces broke on her old ones. These were much more practical and comfortable as far as she was concerned. She hadn't quite gotten the courage to take Miss Sadie up on the offer to make her a pair of moccasins, even though Fannie sang their praises regularly.

Toni slipped out of the wagon and into the darkness of the sleeping camp. Only a few small fires burned and only guards remained awake. "Where are you going, Miss Toni?" Andrew Shewmate asked.

"Are you watching over me tonight, Mr. Shewmate?" Toni had difficulty hiding her irritation. Honestly, it was ridiculous the way Sam insisted she be doubly guarded.

"Yes, Miss. And you know I can't let you wander around camp alone."

"Oh, I'm not. I'm just going to find Mr. Kelley."

"Grant's off patrolling tonight."

Frustration rolled over her. "How long will he be gone?"

"All night, I imagine."

"Listen, I have to go see Mr. Tanner. Are you going to give me any trouble?"

"No." His eyes scanned her face and there was no mistaking the sincerity.

"Good. I'll see you when I return."

"Nope."

"What are you talking about?"

"I'm coming with you."

"I declare," she muttered. "I might as well be a prisoner."

"I think that's what we're trying to keep from happening, Miss Toni." He fell into step beside her, unapologetically.

The quiet admonishment in his tone shamed Toni. "I suppose I should be grateful anyone cares about keeping me safe, but I just don't believe there's a threat that the Cheyenne will be back. We've gone too far now."

"Best we leave supposin' about Indians to those who know best."

Now the incorrigible man was just irritating. "Well, I suppose that's easy to say when you're not the one being followed around every second by a man you hardly know."

"Sorry, Miss Toni. I'm just doin' what I was told. If you'd have brought Ginger with you I wouldn't have to follow you."

"Ginger's been snoring for four hours."

"Well then, I got no choice."

"Then you'd best come on, because I'm going to speak with Blake."

Toni hesitated outside of Blake and Fannie's tent before mustering up the courage to call out. "Fannie! Blake!"

Immediately she heard stirring inside and stepped back to wait. "Toni?" Fannie hissed through the canvas. "Is that you?"

"Yes. I'm sorry to wake you up. I need to speak to you both about Amanda."

"Does it have to be tonight? Blake's sleeping."

Toni scowled and planted her hands on her hips. "Yes, it has to be right now. Don't you think I figured he was sleeping? It's important."

"I'm up," Blake groused. "Don't throw a fit, Toni."

"I'm not!"

They appeared directly. Blake didn't look at all happy, and when he spoke, he didn't even try to hide his irritation. "What is it that couldn't wait until morning?"

"Amanda is in terrible pain and Grant refuses to give her anything to ease it."

"That doesn't sound like Grant," Fannie said. "Are you certain you didn't misunderstand?"

"I'm certain."

"But Grant's usually the first one to want to help when anyone is hurt."

"Not this time." Toni felt Fannie's words like a betrayal. "Perhaps he has something against grieving widows."

"Stop supposing. Both of you." Blake raked his fingers through thick black hair. "I know why he won't give her anything. And I happen to agree with him."

Fannie stared up at her husband. "What do you mean?"

Blake hesitated.

"Tell us," Fannie demanded.

He shrugged his muscular shoulders. "The woman is what's vulgarly referred to as an opium eater."

Outrage filled Toni. "That is beyond ridiculous." But somehow, all the listlessness and slurred speech, desire to sleep, disorientation when she was awake; it all made sense if she were taking too much laudanum.

"Wait a minute," Fannie said. "What's an opium eater?"

Toni turned to her. "Exactly what it sounds like. Someone addicted to opium. Mostly in the form of laudanum."

"You mean medicine?" Fannie's incredulous voice only reminded Toni how far removed she was from decent women. Even Fannie, with her indentured past, had been sheltered from most of the world's depravity. Toni had seen too many prostitutes using the stuff to dull their wits in order to perform for their male customers night after night.

"Yes, Fannie," Toni replied. "The same medicine that dulls pain dulls the senses, and for some people enough use causes them to want more and more."

"You seem to know an awful lot about it," Blake said, that old familiar sneer on his face.

"Yes I do." She faced off with him, unwilling to allow him to make her feel any lower than she already felt. "Now, what's this about Amanda? I have never seen her take anything."

"Tell that to Charles Harrison."

"What's Charles got to do with anything?"

"The reason he's still laid up in his wagon letting his children drive the team is because the bottle of laudanum Amanda had in her apron pocket broke when he threw her on the ground and put out the fire."

"That's what he had sticking in his stomach?"

"What did you think it was?"

"I thought a sharp rock or stick."

"Well, you thought wrong. And now a good man is injured." He shoved his finger toward her. "That woman is not to receive one drop. Is that understood?"

"But she's crying in pain, Blake. How do we ease her pain if she's not allowed laudanum?"

"The burns aren't that bad. Not pleasant for sure, but not severe enough to risk it."

"I'm sorry, Toni." Fannie placed her hand on Toni's arm. "I have to agree with Blake this time. Amanda has been behaving strangely and has scared Katie a couple of times thinking she's Becca. I sympathize with all Amanda's had to endure, but we can't take a chance that she might be a danger to someone."

Toni knew she was outnumbered. And truly, she didn't blame them. Thinking back to the times Amanda seemed listless and unresponsive, she knew Grant's diagnosis was right.

"Why didn't Grant simply tell me?"

"We decided to let her get away from the effects with as few people knowing as possible. Mrs. Kane is a good woman and has been through a lot," Blake said. "There's no point in having people gossip."

"Grant said it shouldn't take too many days to clear her body of all of the effects of the medicine," Blake said, speaking a little more gently than before. "In the meantime, now you know what she's going through so you might help her remember that she'll be better soon."

Toni nodded. "I'm sorry to have wakened you."

Fannie reached forward and wrapped her arms around

Toni. "You're a good friend. Amanda is blessed that you came into her life. Just like I am. Right Blake?"

Toni cringed. Why must Fannie constantly try to bring Blake around? The man would never like her. It was time for Fannie to accept the fact and be grateful that he didn't forbid Fannie to be her friend.

"Well, Blake?"

Toni touched her friend's arm. "It's all right, Fannie."

"No it isn't. If it weren't for you we'd likely still be in Hawkins, Kansas, in that terrible life."

Fannie had to know that wasn't true. If anything it was the other way around. The girl had hidden things away and planned her escape for over a year. Toni joined the effort at the last minute. But when stubborn Fannie got something in her head, there was no telling her anything.

Toni shook her head at poor Blake and gave a little shrug of surrender. He may as well give in too if he wanted to get any sleep at all for the rest of the night. He must have understood her signals, because he gave a large sigh. "Fine. You're a lucky woman to have a friend like Toni. Satisfied?"

Fannie crossed her arms over her chest. "That didn't sound very convincing. Why must you always be so stubborn where Toni's concerned?"

Toni's patience gave out. "Goodnight, you two."

"Wait Toni . . . Blake has something to say."

Weary of the argument, Toni held up a silencing hand. "Fannie. Why make the man tell a lie? If he doesn't want to like me, let him not like me. I'm used to it. Truly, I'm grateful to him for allowing us to join the train. I'm grateful that he came after us with Sam and Grant and brought us back, and I'm grateful that he loves you so much. Beyond that, let the man alone and be a good wife to him. He deserves that much. Now I'm finished here. I'm tired and I just learned bad news about a dear friend. Goodnight." She spun on her heel, leaving Fannie and Blake staring she knew, but she just didn't have the heart to listen to them bicker in front of her any more.

Sam awoke with a start and sat up quickly as Toni flounced by, followed by Andrew Shewmate, who scrambled to keep up. Toni was obviously upset, a circumstance that didn't sit well with Sam. He slid on his moccasins and hurried after them. In a few short strides, he caught up. He clapped Andrew on the shoulder. "It's all right. I'll walk her back to her wagon."

"Better be careful walking alone with me in the middle of the night," Toni said, the sarcasm in her tone completely out of character. "I might feel compromised, then you'd have to marry me."

"Toni, please . . ."

"Please?" she stopped short and whipped about to face him. Anger flashed in her eyes. "Please pretend that kiss between us never happened? Please pretend that you haven't spoken more than two words to me in the week you've been back? Or wait. Maybe you mean, please don't have any feelings about the fact that you've brought a pregnant Indian woman into camp. An Indian woman who appears to be preparing to be your wife." She folded her arms across her chest. "Well? Which one were you referring to?"

"Please do not be angry with me."

Her shoulders slumped and her face crumpled. Sam reached forward, but she stopped him with a palm to his chest. "Don't take me in your arms," she whispered through trembling lips. "It's too hard when you let go."

She turned and walked away. Sam followed. "Please don't follow me, Sam. I can make it back safely from here. You know I can. There are no less than four guards between me and the wagon."

"You do not want me to see you safely to your wagon?"

"No, Sam. I don't," she said over her shoulder. "Goodnight."

Sam watched her until she reached her wagon and ducked inside her tent. He noted both guards standing watch. Satisfied that she was looked after, he turned back toward his own bedroll.

Pain squeezed his heart as he lay close enough to the fire to accept its warmth, but not so close he might end up with worse burns than Mrs. Kane. The hurt in Toni's eyes had nearly done him in. He wanted to ask her to be his wife. His mind raced with the possibilities. But how could they ever be together in this world where the color of a man's skin defined him in so many eyes?

Maybe he was nothing more than a coward.

Twenty-Three

Toni opened her eyes to find Amanda kneeling next to her. "What's wrong? You scared me half to death."

"Shh," her friend smiled and pointed to the sleeping Ginger. "Let's not wake her up. I'm feeling so much better. I want a bath. Will you come with me?"

Something didn't feel right. "Amanda, are you sure you should be getting those burns in water just yet?"

Waving away her concerns, Amanda let out a small laugh. "I'm willing to risk it because I think the water will soothe the stinging," she whispered. "Besides, it's been so long since I've had a bath, I'm afraid people are going to mistake me for Ginger when they smell me coming."

A smile played at the corners of Toni's lips. "I'd love to go with you, but the guards won't let me leave camp without Sam's permission."

"You get dressed. I'll take care of the guards."

Though dubious, Toni shrugged. "You can try if you want."

By the time Toni was dressed, Amanda had returned. "All set?"

"Should we wake Ginger and have her come with us?"

"Let her sleep. She's going to be scouting all day tomorrow. Plus I've noticed she's been coughing. She should probably not come out by the water at night."

Toni had noticed the cough too. Amanda had a point. She nodded. "What did you do with the guards?"

"Promised to use the last of my jarred apples and bake them a pie if they'd let us go to the creek so I could have a bath before the whole camp wakes up."

"They agreed to leave their posts for a pie?" Toni was almost insulted at the lack of loyalty from the men who were supposed to be her protectors. She almost suspected Amanda of lying, but when she stepped outside, not one guard stood there to order her back inside or walk with her wherever she was going.

A feeling of nakedness overwhelmed her. And the image of Swooping Eagle's face haunted her.

"Amanda, wait." Her friend turned.

"What's wrong?"

"Nothing really. I just . . . I don't think we should go alone."

"Oh, Toni. Don't be a chicken." Her voice sounded trembly, as though she might burst into tears. "You said you'd go with me."

"Are you sure you're up to this?" Toni asked.

"Toni, please!" Her voice rose slightly. "I-I have to do this."

"All right. I'm sorry." Amanda probably did crave the cool water on her legs. And after all the sweating and pain she'd endured, a nice bath would likely hit the spot.

The two women remained as quiet as possible as they left the campsite and wandered toward the creek. There were more rocks and less trees in this part of the country and not too many places to hide while undressing. So when they reached the creek, Toni looked around. "All right. You get undressed, I'll stand guard."

Amanda whipped around and grabbed Toni by the arms. The wild look in her eyes scared the fire out of Toni. "What's wrong?" she asked.

"Toni, I can't do this to you. You have to get back to camp, right now."

"You aren't making any sense."

A sob caught in Amanda's throat. "The two men that went with Sam. They must have overheard someone talking about the laudanum. They came to my tent last night while you were gone and said if I'd bring you to the woods, they'd give me some. And even had a little for me as sort of a down payment."

Amanda's words began to sink in and fear shot through her. That explained why the woman had stopped sobbing and had fallen into a blissful sleep by the time Toni returned to her tent.

"Let's get back to camp," she said, disgusted with Amanda but glad she'd decided to tell the truth before it was too late. She whipped around as Amanda screamed.

"Don't give us any trouble, lady." Tim, the man who had lost his wife and daughter, held her fast. He glanced at Amanda. "Here's your pay." He shoved a bottle into her hands.

Amanda shoved it back. "No. No, take it back. Let her go. Please, let her go."

Anger shot through Toni as she registered the betrayal. She'd been sold out for what? A bottle of medicine?

"Toni, I'm sorry. I'm so sorry."

"I don't understand. What do you men want with me?"

"Not what you're thinking, dirty whore."

Amanda's sobs were growing louder. "Toni, please say you forgive me."

"All right. Amanda, I forgive you."

"No. You couldn't. They're going to . . ."

"What? What are they going to do?" Toni's heart began to beat wildly in her chest as her suspicion grew.

"They're taking you to that Indian. He told Sam he'd let the other captives go in exchange for you."

Toni's body went all at once hot and cold. "You're taking me to the Cheyenne?" Her gaze lifted to meet Tim's but he refused to look her in the eye.

"I got no choice if I'm to get my little girl back."

"But I thought the soldiers were going to go in and demand their return."

"That's what they say," Brian answered. "But by the time the army gets there, it might be too late. I can't take a chance on my sister being there any longer. All we got to do is deliver you to Swooping Eagle and we get our loved ones back."

Even to Toni, it sounded logical. Why not trade a whore

for three beautiful females who had full wonderful lives ahead of them? Somehow, it made sense.

"All right. Did you think to steal a horse for me?"

"You ain't gonna fight us?" Tim asked.

Toni shook her head. "What's the use?"

"We got horses hid a half a mile downstream."

"Then let's go."

"What about her?" Tim asked nodding toward Amanda.

"Let her go. She's already got half that bottle gone. She ain't a threat," commanded Brian.

Tim shook his head in disgust. "All right. Let's go."

"Over my dead body."

Toni nearly wept with relief at the sound of Ginger's familiar hoarse voice. "You two men drop your guns to the ground and kick 'em aside."

"Don't even try to keep us from taking her, girlie." Tim snarled and tried to grab onto Toni, but she dodged him and ran to Ginger's side.

"I'm not trying, I'm doin'. If you don't do as I say, I'm gonna have to shoot. And don't think I won't. Now, do you want your little girl to be an orphan? Or do you want to be here when the army brings her back?"

"Better do as she says, men."

Sam and Grant walked toward them guns drawn. Brian and Tim relented.

"How'd you two know?" Ginger asked.

Sam spoke to Ginger, but kept his eyes on Toni. She was just so grateful to be rescued, it was all she could do not to throw herself into Sam's arms. "Yellow Bird saw Mrs. Kane leading her out of here and assumed the two men had found someone else to betray you."

"Betray me?" Toni asked. Her body began to shake.

"First, they thought Yellow Bird would want to get you out of the way. So they went to her with the proposition that she lure you away from the wagon train where they would kidnap you and take you to Swooping Eagle."

Sam couldn't wait any longer and he reached for Toni and pulled her into the warmth of his arms. Mindless of the stares of the people around, she nestled into his chest, enjoying the comfort for however long it lasted.

"Why would they think Yellow Bird wanted to get me out of the way?"

He gave a short laugh and pulled back. "Apparently, I am unable to hide the way I feel about you from anyone but you."

Toni hesitated. "What are you saying exactly?"

"That I'm through fighting my love for you. I'm asking you to marry me."

"It's about time you got some sense in that thick head of yours."

"Ginger, please," Toni said. Couldn't she even get a proposal without Ginger butting in?

"All right, I'm gonna get these two idiots back to camp before they hurt someone." She looked at Grant and jerked her head toward Amanda. "You'd best go get her. You'll probably have to carry her back to camp."

"What do you think will happen to Amanda?" Toni asked.

"She needs help. You don't think Blake will force her to leave the train, do you?"

Sam tightened his arms around her. "I don't know. Blake will want to speak with her and there will most likely be ramifications for these actions. But perhaps he will be lenient since her heart is in so much pain."

"Oh, I hope so."

Brian's eyes flashed with raw hatred. "I hope you know you've probably condemned my sister to life as a squaw."

"As you were about to do to Toni," Sam said grimly. "However, the soldiers should be arriving at the camp of Swooping Eagle any day to try to negotiate their release. I do not think the Cheyenne are ready for a war."

"You'd best be right," Tim said. His voice broke. "This isn't fair."

"I know," Sam said, his voice filled with kindness. "But we can't trade one person for another."

"I don't know how you can compare that woman to my little girl."

"You were wrong when you said we should trade Toni to Swooping Eagle because there was no one who cared about her."

Sam took Toni's hand and laced her fingers with his. "I love this woman with my whole heart and I wouldn't give her up to save a thousand lives." He spoke with such conviction, Toni's heart nearly burst with pride.

"All right," Ginger said, firmly. "Enough of this jawin'. I'm getting' them back to camp and you two have unfinished business."

Sam's fingers remained curled around Toni's as they watched until the others were out of sight. Then he turned to her. "Well?"

"You're waiting for an answer?"

"You know I am."

"What about Yellow Bird?"

"I had thought I might make the offer of marriage to her," he admitted, sending shards of pain through Toni's heart at the very thought of losing Sam to another woman. "We are both Indian. It would have been easy for society to accept such a marriage. But even Yellow Bird knew it would not be the right thing between us. She came to me tonight and spoke from her heart. She could see how much I love you and did not want to be the reason I wasn't with the woman I love."

"I see." Toni truly didn't know what else to say. She stared out at the eastern horizon where the darkness was beginning to fade over the mountains. "It's beautiful, isn't it?"

Sam unlaced their fingers and wrapped his arm around her waist. He stared into her eyes as he drew her closer and closer. "Oregon is even more beautiful. The valleys are lush and the land wide open for planting. I dream of building a mission there for the tribes. To teach them about Jesus and perhaps eventually open a school."

Toni's heart sank, as clarity once more invaded her mind. She could never be with Sam. She was still a former prostitute and he had his heart set on preaching. God surely wouldn't want him marrying someone like her. "You'll be wonderful, Sam."

His brow creased. "But . . . ?"

"But there's still a problem."

"What's that?" his eyes searched hers. "You don't love me?"

"You know I do." Tears filled Toni's eyes. "You said we couldn't be together because of my past."

"I'm sure I never said anything like that."

"Yes, you did. I heard you speaking to Blake not long ago. You said you didn't see how a marriage could ever work between us."

Dumbfounded, Sam stared.

"You see? You can't even deny it."

"You heard that?"

Toni nodded. The warmth of Sam's arms felt too good to walk away, even if he was about to take back the proposal.

"Why did you think that had anything to do with your past?"

That wasn't exactly the explanation she was looking for. Instead, she had to be the one to explain. "B-because—well, what else could it be?"

Sam's eyes filled with tenderness and he pulled her closer. "I'm going to kiss you." And his lips pressed to hers. Toni's arms slipped around his neck as she returned kiss for kiss. His arms and lips evoked feelings she'd never known. She felt like a giddy schoolgirl as his love for her drove the thought of every man who had used her from her mind.

Sam pulled away and took her hands in his. He pressed them to his chest and demanded her gaze. "Don't you know I mean it when I say you are pure and clean before God?" Sam asked, his brown eyes filled with earnest devotion. "I would never be the one to make you feel as though you were still the woman that lived above George's Saloon. You are in all ways new and chaste. In God's eyes and mine."

Toni's heart was so full, a burst of laughter flooded her. Then she stopped.

"Then what did you mean?" she whispered. "When you said a marriage could never work between us?"

He smiled and pressed his warm, soft lips to her forehead, "What I meant was that I am half Indian and you are a white woman."

Toni felt her jaw drop. Then anger hit her. "Do you mean to tell me that you almost didn't ask me to marry you because people wouldn't like a white woman to be married to a half Indian man?"

He smiled, but nodded. "That's exactly right."

"God looks at the heart, and so do I. I never thought about you being an Indian except for how handsome you are."

"I'm glad my appearance pleases you." He gave her a quick kiss, then pulled away again. "We're bound to face some difficulty eventually because I'm half Sioux. So weigh your decision carefully before you answer."

Stubbornness squared Toni's shoulders and raised her chin. She looked Sam full in the eyes. "I've already answered."

"You have?"

"Haven't I?" Toni frowned, her mind going over every word they'd spoken. "Perhaps I haven't. Then let me tell you why I want to marry you." She lifted her face and gave him a brief kiss. "Because this is the second time you've come to my rescue. The first time you came after me when George kidnapped me, and you brought me back. The second time you came after me before these two could even take me away."

Sam pressed his finger to her lips. "And from now on, I'll never let you go in the first place. If you'll answer the question. Will you marry me?"

Toni closed her eyes, reveling in how safe she felt in Sam's strong and capable arms. "Kiss me, and you'll have my answer."

The years of heartache melted away in the promise of this man's love. She knew she had nothing to fear. Nothing from the past could touch her now. And in Sam's eyes she felt truly beautiful. In his arms she knew that God had truly swept away her destroyed past and ahead was a life of beauty and happiness with the man God had created for her.

Toni's eyes filled with tears as Sam gently pressed his lips to hers. She kissed him back in a way that she prayed left no doubt in his mind that she was going to be his bride.

Dear Readers,

The theme of Beauty for Ashes never fails to amaze and draw me. Like so many of you, I have areas in my past that still bring me pain. But God is unwavering in faithfulness, constantly reminding me of his grace, mercy, and unfailing love for me. Like Toni, I've many times felt scarred, ugly, unworthy of love, and many times I've pulled away from the very arms that tried to reach out to me, both human and heavenly. I'm so glad that God sees us for who we truly are. Deep down in a place that only He knows about. And he never, ever gives up. Brokenness draws his compassion and He'll never ignore an honest cry.

In *Distant Heart* I addressed not only my heroine's need to surrender her past to God and accept his grace once and for all, but also other people's perception of her based on her past. Other Christians who found it so difficult to give her the benefit of the doubt. Just as I see myself in Toni, sadly, I often see myself in those who judge her as well.

If there's one thing I pray, it's that we, as Christians would open our hearts and arms to the men and women who walk into the church wounded, battered and in desperate need of a kind word or gentle embrace. I think Jesus could do so much more on the earth, if we could stop defining the lost by the scars they display. Perhaps not be so afraid of loving those we fear—not fear physically, but maybe we're afraid to see a little of ourselves in the unlovely, the prostitute, the adulterer, the alcoholic. Because never has it been truer that only grace separates me from the stripper in a little dive who is trying to make a living for her children, or the prostitute who ran away from an abusive home and somehow has to survive on the streets because that's better than the alternative. The alcoholic or drug addict who never meant to become so dependent on the one thing that numbed the pain.

Only Jesus can save.

I pray as you read this that God reminded you His great love goes beyond the things you've done. Beyond what you do. His mercy and grace never change and his love never fails. May He exchange beauty for the hurt and ashes of your past. And shower you with hope for a bright tomorrow. Remember your best days are yet to come.

Until next time, may God bless you richly and make His face shine upon you.

Tracey Bateman

Discussion Questions

1. In the beginning, Toni feels her outward scars will make people see her differently, perhaps make them forget about her past. What does God say truly matters? Have there been instances when you felt your suffering somehow made you more acceptable to God? Less?

2. Toni doesn't feel like she's good enough for Sam because of his relationship with God. When have you felt that you didn't measure up spiritually to another Christian? How did you overcome the tendency to compare yourself to others?

3. Fannie's friendship with Toni is true and real, but she's constantly battling Blake because of his opinion of Toni. How might that have backfired? What would God expect of Fannie in this situation?

4. Ginger is surly and rude at times, and yet Toni continues to be her friend. Has God ever brought someone into your life like this? Were you willing to love against all reason? Would you?

5. Do you know someone who is suffering from scars of a sinful past? How do those scars manifest themselves? Are you willing to be God's hands to reach out in love?

6. Amanda Kane chooses to dull her pain with a drug. Have you or someone you've known ever done the same thing? How do we as a body of Christ help other believers who are dealing with addiction? What are some common ways people medicate themselves against pain?

7. Sam's assumption that he isn't right for Toni because he's half Indian brings the race issue into the book. How do you see this issue? We know that the Israelites were forbidden to marry anyone of a different race that might introduce false gods or religions in their midst, but what, if anything, does God, in the New Testament, have to say about intermarrying?

8. Tim and Brian were desperate to retrieve their loved ones, so much so that they were willing to trade Toni to accomplish their goals. They saw Toni as less valuable as a person because of her past. Have you ever considered others as less because of where they come from or because you can see their sin on the outside?

9. If a known ex-prostitute came to your church, how do you think you would respond? Disgust? Fear? Compassion? Mercy?

10. The book's theme deals with beauty for ashes. Are you struggling with a past that still causes you pain? Do you feel like you need God to heal those hurts? Can you ask for prayer?

Turn the page for an exciting preview of

DANGEROUS HEART

The final book in the Westward Hearts series
By Tracey Bateman
Coming Soon from Avon Inspire

A blast of gunfire startled Ginger Freeman from the first sound sleep she'd had in a week. She bolted upright in the tent she shared with Toni Rodden and fumbled around in the dark for her moccasins.

"What is it?" Toni asked from the other side of the tent. She made a shadowy figure as she sat up and reached for her own shoes.

"I don't know. I'm going to check on it." She slipped on her moccasins and stood to her feet. "You best stay put."

Another blast of gunfire pierced the air and the sound of yelling echoed through the camp. "Outlaws! Take cover!"

Toni gasped.

"Outlaws?" Ginger frowned. "What kind of dumb outlaws would attack a wagon train the size of this one?"

"Maybe there's a lot of them." Toni's voice trembled, but Ginger didn't have time to coddle her friend. She figured her help was needed out there. After all, she could shoot just as straight and just as fast as any man—just about.

"I ain't ever heard of any outlaws traveling in a band that big."

And if there was one thing Ginger knew a little something about, it was outlaws. Of course, she couldn't very well mention that fact to Toni or anyone else, but this attack just didn't make any kind of sense. There were either an awful lot of men who thought there was an awful lot of treasure to be had among this battered, weary band of travelers, or the men out there firing into the camp were missing a few brains. That's what Ginger was betting on.

"I'll be back as soon as I can," she said to Toni. "Hunker down and stay out of sight."

Ginger pulled back the tent flap and slipped outside, taking care to keep her head down and her senses alert. She gripped her Colt revolver firmly in her right hand, ready to use it if necessary, and she figured it would be necessary real soon.

She tried to take stock of the situation. Outside the circle of wagons, the trees were thick enough to hide a few outlaws bent on mischief. But she still couldn't imagine anyone dumb enough to go up against a wagon train the size of this one. Dawn was beginning to break over the mountains to the east, but it was still too dark to make out more than shadows beyond the camp's fires.

Strong fingers gripped her buckskin-clad arm and spun her around. Grant Kelley stood there, a deep frown pushing his eyebrows together. "Ginger, get back inside that tent before you get your head shot off!"

"My gun's as good as yours, Grant Kelley, so mind your own business."

"You're too bullheaded for your own good." Grant yanked her to the ground with him as a bullet whizzed past her ear. Ducking behind a wagon wheel, he took aim in the direction that bullet had come from and fired off two shots, then turned back to her. "Remember last time you joined a man's fight, you got an arrow through your leg."

Humiliation burned her cheeks at the low-down reminder that he had been the one to pull that arrow out and patch her up while she laid on the ground in a dead faint. She took aim toward the trees, firing off a couple of rounds herself. "I'll be sure not to get in the way of a bullet."

"See that you don't." He fired again. And again.

Not to be outdone, Ginger raised her Colt toward the woods and squeezed the trigger. "Ow!" she heard a split second later. "Dadburn it, I just got myself shot! Fall back."

Ginger gave a smug grin. "See how he likes that," she said. Then on a whim she called out, "Keep your head down if you don't want to get it shot off." Then it occurred to her Grant had said the same thing to her less than ten minutes earlier. Her face warmed and she hoped he didn't remember that he'd said it first.

Grant snorted. "That was luck."

Outraged at the very suggestion, Ginger turned a fierce glare on the wagon scout. "What are you talking about? I aimed plain as the nose on your face, Grant Kelley."

He fired off a round. "No one could see into those woods.

There's no shame in getting a luck shot. I'd venture to say that's the first bullet to make contact with one of those varmints."

"I'd say so too," Ginger said stubbornly. "Only it wasn't a lucky shot. I took aim."

Within minutes it seemed all the outlaws figured out they were fighting a losing battle. The gunfire stopped and, by the rustling in the trees, it was apparent they had ridden away. Ginger doubted they'd be back. Slowly, cautiously, the members of the wagon train stood and ventured out.

"Doc!" someone called. Ginger looked up at Grant. "They're callin for you."

His eyes clouded over. "I wish they wouldn't call me that."

"How come? That's what you are."

"Was."

He looked past her, and Ginger turned to find thirteen-year-old Katie Caldwell running toward them. "Doc! Miss Sadie says come quick. Yellow Bird's time has come and she's having a rough go of it."

"I'll be right there!" Grant turned to Ginger and placed his big hands on her shoulders. "Go to the supply wagon and bring the black doctor bag to Miss Sadie's tent. It's on the right when you go in. Hurry up. You know if Miss Sadie called for me, something must be wrong."

Ginger didn't argue. Nor did she speak. Instead, she nodded and took off at a run to do as she'd been instructed.

Grant entered Miss Sadie's tent without waiting to be invited. Yellow Bird, the young Indian woman who had joined the wagon train only recently, writhed in pain, but didn't utter a sound.

"What seems to be the trouble?" he asked the middle-aged widow, whose face was drawn with worry. Miss Sadie had helped with the birthing of every baby born in the wagon train since they headed out from Independence almost four months earlier.

"I think the baby is stuck."

"How long has she been having pains?"

"Since yesterday afternoon."

Grant examined her and found Miss Sadie's assessment of the situation to be correct. He nodded to Miss Sadie. "You're right," he said grimly. "I need to pray."

He took Yellow Bird's hand. She stared up at him, eyes filled with pain and fear. "My baby?"

"We need to get him out soon or he'll die." Grant reached forward and smoothed a strand of silky black hair from her forehead. "Do you know Jesus?"

Yellow Bird nodded. "I know Him."

"Okay, then we're going to pray that God will help me deliver your baby safely."

He kept her hand firmly inside of his and they closed their eyes just as Ginger barreled in, her eyes wild, chest heaving from exertion. "Here's the bag. How is she?" She looked down at Yellow Bird. "You okay?"

The Indian woman nodded. "We will pray now."

Grant looked up at Ginger. Her face was void of all color and it was easy to see the worry in her eyes.

"Well, I suppose I'll just wait outside 'til you're done."

"Sit down, Ginger," Grant said, irritation edging his voice. "Close your eyes and be quiet while we pray."

Yellow Bird nodded, her teary eyes filled with pleading as she looked up at Ginger. "You pray too. For my ba-by."

Ginger's face gentled more than Grant had ever seen before. To her credit she knelt beside Yellow Bird. Then she opened her mouth. "Okay, but God ain't never answered any of my prayers before," she muttered. "I don't see why He'd start now."

Grant nudged her. She nodded a little as though she understood his meaning. "I bet this is my lucky day, though," she hastily (and poorly in Grant's opinion) tried to amend.

"Let's hope," Grant said. They bowed their heads and he began to pray. "Lord, give me wisdom and mercy to bring this baby safely into your beautiful world. Show me how to dislodge the baby's head and bring it forth. Amen."

Ginger spoke with matter-of-fact confidence. "When our old cow was having a rough go of it one time, my daddy reached in and turned the little calf and yanked on it a little. It came out neat as you please."

Grant rubbed Yellow Bird's belly, hoping the baby would dislodge itself from wherever it seemed to be hung up. "Well, a calf isn't a baby."

"Well, I know that," Ginger said, scowling. "Don't you think I know the difference?"

Yellow Bird moaned. Grant knew she had to be in excruciating pain; still she barely made a sound.

He caught Miss Sadie's gaze. Dark circles surrounded her

eyes and the lines on her face seemed more pronounced than he'd ever noticed. "You might give Ginger's suggestion a try, Grant," she said. "I've seen it work on more babies than I can count."

Still, Grant hesitated. How could he bear it if the child died in his hands, along with Yellow Bird. "It's risky."

"But not impossible," she countered.

He nodded, then turned to the young mother. "Yellow Bird," he said softly, caressing her sweat-soaked brow. "Your baby is not able to come any further because he isn't in the right position. I am going to try to turn him and pull him out. It will be painful, and there are no guarantees. But we have to try. Do you understand?"

She moaned and nodded.

Grant sprang into action. The young woman was growing weaker by the minute and if he didn't do something fast he would likely lose them both. "Ginger, Miss Sadie, get on either side of Yellow Bird and don't let her thrash about too much."

"Me?" Ginger's voice sounded faint. "Uh, I'll just go get Toni or Fannie. And I'll be right back."

"There's no time!" Grant grabbed the white-faced girl by the shoulders and gave her a little shake. "Ginger! You have to be strong. I know you don't like illness or blood. But you can*not* faint, is that clear?"

"Wh-who said I was going to faint?"

Good—some of her spunk was showing.

Grant tried not to be affected by the sound of Yellow

Bird's groans as he felt for the baby's head and slowly began to turn it to the right position. Still, with the next pain, the baby didn't descend any further.

Ginger prayed the same two words over an over like a mantra. "Please God, please God, please God, please God." Finally, Grant's nerves couldn't take it any longer.

"Ginger! Shut up."

"Well, you're the one that told me to pray!"

"Can't you pray something else?"

Yellow Bird let out a scream that pierced the interior of the tent.

Ginger resumed her prayer. "Please God, please God, please God, please God."

As Grant felt the baby begin to dislodge, he found himself praying Ginger's prayer. "Please God, please God, please God."

Moments later, a healthy boy slid into the world with lusty cries. "Would you look at that?" Ginger said, excitement and wonder in her tone. Miss Sadie wrapped the baby and tried to give him to Yellow Bird. The young woman had fainted. "Ginger, take the baby," Miss Sadie said. "I need to help Grant take care of Yellow Bird."

"I might drop it," Ginger said. "I never held a human baby before."

"It's okay, honey," Miss Sadie said. "There's nothing to it."

Miss Sadie slipped the baby carefully into Ginger's arms. A soft gasp caused Grant to raise his head just for a second. Surprise lifted his brow. For all of her spit and fire, and annoying behavior, Ginger Freeman could be as soft as any woman when holding a baby.

Special Thanks

My family: Rusty, Cat, Mike, Stevan, and Will. You give me grace and space to do what I do. Thank you for so graciously sharing my dream. I share each of yours as well.

Mom, as always, your support means everything to me.

Chris, Kevin, Kristianna, and Kaleigh Lynxwiler. God breathes his goodness through you. Your commitment to Christ constantly inspires me to check my heart. I love each of you as cherished family members. Thank you for your unconditional love, kindness, and friendship.

Cindy DiTiberio. You have great insights that I appreciate so much. You've truly made the editing process a team effort and I value our partnership. I pray that God will continue to bless you in your career and give you wisdom to continue the job He's given you to do for His glory.

The HarperSanFrancisco/Avon Inspire team from marketing to cover design to every other area that I know very little about but recognize from the results. I'm in awe of your incredible work on this series. Every detail is attended to in such a caring manner. I'm extremely thankful that you hold my books in your hands and do everything you can to join with me to get them to the readers.

Last, but most definitely not least, my agent Steve Laube. I thank my God upon every remembrance of you. Thank you for understanding me, even though you may need therapy if you stick with me much longer. I'll split the cost with you.

Tracey Bateman

Tracey Bateman lives in Missouri with her husband and four children. Their rural home provides a wonderful atmosphere for a writer's imagination to grow and produce characters, plots, and settings. In 1994, with three children to raise, she and her husband agreed that she should go to college and earn a degree. In a freshman English class, her love for writing was rekindled and she wrote a short story that she later turned into a book. Her college career was cut short with the news of their fourth baby's impending arrival, but the seeds of hope for a writing career had already taken root. Over the next several years she wrote, hooked up with critique partners, studied the craft of writing, and eventually all the hard work paid off.

She currently has over twenty-five books published in a variety of genres. Tracey believes completely that God has big plans for His kids, and that all things are possible to those who will put their hope and trust in Him.

Jennifer Probst brings the "nonstop sexual tension" (Laura Kaye) that lights up her *New York Times* and *USA Today* bestsellers to a dazzling new series of a matchmaking agency where love's magic is at work!

SEARCHING FOR PERFECT

"Entertaining and engaging and real. . . . Jennifer Probst is a romance writing superstar. . . . [A] fantastic series."

—*Bella's Little Book Blog*

"A wonderfully moving, deeply emotional, steamy, sexy, fantastic story of hope, healing, and love. 5 huge loving stars!"

—*Sizzling Book Club*

SEARCHING FOR SOMEDAY

"A sophisticated, sexy romance . . . witty, passionate."
—*RT Book Reviews*

"Refreshing."

—*Publishers Weekly*

"Full of emotion and heart. . . . 5 stars!"
—*Sizzling Book Club*

"Delightfully romantic and fun. . . . One of the best contemporary authors!"

—*Under the Covers*

"Offers both heat and heart."

—*Booklist Online*